"To our new partnership," he said, his voice a sensual growl of anticipation that immediately created answering ripples in the pit of her stomach.

Determined to quell them, she snapped, "Are you always so openly provocative?"

He broke the tension with a sudden laugh. "I've never met another woman quite so woundingly honest! I can't help it, I'm afraid. Some men are born to it, while others need to be coaxed out of their shell by a loving, sensitive hand."

Kira felt color riot in her cheeks. Before she could explode, Stefano turned his statement into a warning.

"I am most definitely *not* one of those men."

CHRISTINA HOLLIS was born a few miles from Bath, England. She began writing as soon as she could hold a pencil, but was always told to concentrate on getting a "proper" job.

She joined a financial institution straight from school. After some years of bean counting, report writing and partying hard, she reached the heady heights of "gofer" in the marketing department. At that point, a wonderful case of love at first sight led to marriage within months. She was still spending all her spare time writing, and when one of her plays was short-listed in a BBC competition, her husband suggested she try writing full-time.

Half a dozen full-length novels and a lot of nonfiction work for national magazines followed. After a long maternity break, she joined a creative writing course to update her skills. There, she was encouraged to experiment with a form she loved to read but had never tried writing before—romance fiction. Her first Harlequin® Presents title, *The Italian Billionaire's Virgin,* began life as a two-thousand-word college assignment. She thinks that writing romance must be the best job in the world! It gives her the chance to do something she loves while hopefully bringing pleasure to others.

Christina has two lovely children and a cat. She lives on the Welsh border and enjoys reading, gardening and feeding the birds.

Visit her website at www.christinahollis.com.

MASTER OF BELLA TERRA

CHRISTINA HOLLIS

~ FROM RAGS TO RICHES ~

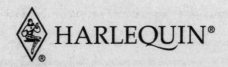

TORONTO • NEW YORK • LONDON
AMSTERDAM • PARIS • SYDNEY • HAMBURG
STOCKHOLM • ATHENS • TOKYO • MILAN • MADRID
PRAGUE • WARSAW • BUDAPEST • AUCKLAND

Recycling programs
for this product may
not exist in your area.

ISBN-13: 978-0-373-52798-4

MASTER OF BELLA TERRA

Previously published in the U.K. under the title
THE ITALIAN'S BLUSHING GARDENER

First North American Publication 2011

Copyright © 2010 by Christina Hollis

MASTER OF BELLA TERRA

CHAPTER ONE

SHADOWS rippled over Kira's slight form. She stood on the lookout of ancient pine trees guarding the Bella Terra estate, all her attention focused on the other side of the valley. Far away across the rolling grassland a white streak scarred the distant hillside. It was a road, and Kira was waiting. She was watching for the telltale cloud of white Tuscan dust that meant the end of her solitude.

Her little patch of paradise was about to be changed for ever. The land surrounding her house was up for sale. And according to Bella Terra's estate agent, the most fantastic man in the world was interested in buying it.

Kira could not have cared less. She had moved to Italy to get away from all that. Everything she had heard so far about Signor Stefano Albani hadn't done anything to improve her general opinion of men. He had been due to view the Bella Terra villa and estate earlier that afternoon, but he hadn't shown up. The female estate agent had called in at Kira's cottage, looking for him. She had been breathless with excitement and full of this charming billionaire's flirty telephone manner, but Kira wasn't impressed. She guessed this rogue Albani was probably more interested in women than he was in buying a big country estate.

As time went on and he still never showed up, the estate agent's interest dwindled. She began to worry about missing her next appointment. Eventually, feeling sorry for her, Kira offered to take care of the villa's keys and details. Dealing with strangers tied her in knots, but it didn't look as though Signor Albani was coming, and her offer was only a ploy anyway. All she really wanted to do was get rid of the estate agent.

It worked. Her unwelcome visitor dashed off, leaving Kira alone once more.

That was exactly how she liked it.

And there were much worse ways of spending an afternoon than enjoying this view of the Bella Terra estate.

The scorching sun eventually slid behind a bank of clouds, heading for the wooded ridge on the western side of the valley. Kira began to relax. She felt more and more confident that Stefano the Seducer wouldn't come. That was a relief to her, in more ways than one. The fewer people who viewed the estate, the longer it would take to sell. Kira didn't care if the rambling old place stayed empty forever. Her small home was nicely isolated from the villa, although each building could see the other in the distance.

Bella Terra's last owner, Sir Ivan, had been as reserved as Kira. They had waved to each other across the valley every day, and she had looked after the estate gardens, but that was pretty much the extent of their friendship. It had suited them both, but now Sir Ivan was dead. It was odd: in the two years since she had bought La Ritirata Kira had rarely spoken to the man except on business, yet she missed him. And now she was faced with the unknown. Whoever bought La Bella Terra was unlikely to be as peaceful and unobtrusive as the old man. She hated that thought.

She wondered if the future would seem quite so threatening if she had someone to talk to. A letter had arrived from England the previous day. Kira knew she should have sent a curt reply by return, but couldn't bear to do it. The envelope lay where she had dropped it, unopened, on the kitchen table. She would have to release its tentacles of emotional blackmail sooner or later, but not just now.

With an effort, she tried to concentrate on the beautiful scene in front of her. The valley was a patchwork of flowery grassland and ancient woods. She strolled as far as the cool green shadows of the sweet chestnut wood. Thunderheads were forming over the hills. There would be a storm soon. That would cool everything down. She smiled. Rain would transform the single-track road leading to the Bella Terra villa into a quagmire. If Signor Albani was still on his way, that was almost guaranteed to put him off. The prospect of fighting a prestige sports car upstream like a salmon was sure to turn him back. Her little retreat would be safe for a while longer.

As Kira counted her blessings, she became aware of a subtle change in the air. All the birds fell silent. She looked around. The landscape was poised, waiting for something to happen. Then she felt a vibration. Faint at first, it rose from the ground beneath her feet like an earthquake. She started forward as a roe deer bounced through the trees behind her. With one bound it crossed the track and was gone. Still the shuddering increased, rising up through Kira's ribcage until she looked around for somewhere to run. Instinctively, she headed out into the summer-rich pasture. The trees surrounding it had been still in the oppressive heat. Now they swayed and bucked like a wild green sea. It wasn't an earthquake, but something even more alarming. A helicopter was sweeping in from above, and tearing Kira's peaceful valley apart.

'I'm going off-message for a couple of hours,' Stefano Albani announced into his hands-free phone. 'I've got the Milan project back on track, and if Murray's people ring, tell them the publishing tie-in is off, unless they come up with something that can really appeal to me.'

Closing the call, he sat back in his seat. There was no question of relaxing; his spine remained rigid. Flying a helicopter took a lot of concentration. He never inspected any property from ground level without making a low-level pass over it first. The Bella Terra estate looked perfect, and its aspect was a dream. Cool, shady woodlands offered sanctuary from the roasting heat of summer, while beautifully planned terraces around the house offered plenty of space for entertaining in the golden sunshine. Talking of which...

A movement at the edge of the trees caught his eye. It was a girl. She was flinging her arms about, and waving papers at him. Stefano's sensuous mouth lifted in a half-smile. He had only spoken to the estate agent by phone so far, but from where he was sitting she looked as good as she sounded.

His dark features eased as he thought back to that long, teasing telephone conversation with her. Taking up where they had left off would be a good way to wind down after a high-pressure day.

He gazed down on the pretty little ragazza, and gave her a wave. As he did so, a corresponding ripple of relief passed up his arm and across his shoulders. His muscles were tense from working for far too long without a break. What he needed was distraction. A few hours in a place like this would take his mind off all those boardroom battles and investment decisions. The company of a pretty girl was a bonus he had half forgotten in all the chaos.

Stefano smiled as he set his helicopter down on the far side of the house. His few precious hours of freedom were off to a great start.

Kira was in no mood for games. Bella Terra was supposed to be a private valley, and the helicopter's racket was shockingly intrusive among all that usually undisturbed beauty. Worst of all, it felt like an omen of things to come.

'I've seen pheasants fly higher than that!' she shouted after the helicopter as it swept overhead. Her voice was totally swamped by the thundering rumble of its rotors, but it hardly mattered. Simply putting her anger into words made Kira feel better.

As she watched, hands on hips, the machine swung its nose around and dropped down behind the beautiful old villa. If the pilot's antics hadn't made her so annoyed, she might have been nervous. Instead, she saw it as a chance to catch up with him. She sprinted along the track, heading for an overgrown entrance to the Bella Terra gardens. Squeezing in through a gap in its rusty ironwork, she marched up the path.

She found the helicopter parked as neatly as a saloon car, very close to the main house. It was deserted, and silent apart from the click of cooling metalwork. There was absolutely no sign of the pilot. Confused, she circled the villa buildings in the sultry heat. From every side, ornamental broom and gorse set off their exploding pods like gunfire. Anyone with any sense would have headed straight for shade. She made for the yew walk. Reaching the north end, she glimpsed a tall, masculine figure disappearing through a gap in the hedge that led into the fountain garden. She was about to call out to him, but something about the decided, athletic grace of his movements made her pause, and when she came out into the sunlit square of the fountain garden, it was empty.

Turning her head, she strained to hear any signs of life. Only the quiet rustle of air through pine trees and the constant sniper fire of genista seeds disturbed the peace. Then, as she listened, she heard something that might have been footsteps. It was only one tiny sound, and all the interconnecting yew hedges made it difficult to decide from which direction it came. She looked around, but there was no one.

Then two strong hands slipped around her waist, and in one smooth movement she was drawn into an inescapable embrace.

'We meet at last, Miss Barrett!' a deep, delicious Italian voice purred in perfect English. 'I have been searching for you. I felt sure you would be waiting for me at Bella Terra's front door!'

His teasing words reverberated into the curve of Kira's neck. She froze, shrinking from the whisper of warm breath against her skin. The movement only drew her closer to his hard, masculine body. He was holding her so perfectly, she could barely breathe.

'When we spoke on the phone you said you were looking forward to meeting me. Remind me—exactly where did you want to have dinner tonight?' There was a soft, low chuckle in his voice as he murmured, pulling her around to ravish her with a kiss.

Before he could make contact, Kira burst from his grasp with reflexes that astonished them both.

'I'm not Amanda Barrett, and I'm not very happy!' she confronted him, breathing fast. 'Please keep your hands to yourself!'

The visitor recoiled instantly, but he was far too professional to give his horror free rein. Instead, his features became a mask. With a slow, careful dip of his head, he addressed her gravely. 'Scusi, signora.'

Glaring, Kira took two steps backwards. His assault had been so swift and sure she hardly expected him to stop so suddenly. She had no idea what to do next. If this was Signor Stefano Albani, billionaire, then he was nothing like any of the rich men she had worked with in the past. They were predictable, humourless and would never have dreamed of such a stunt. In contrast, Stefano Albani looked ready for anything. He was fit and he was handsome in a tense, distracted way. Standing straight and tall before her, he seemed quite unfazed by her rebuff. He brushed his shirtsleeves down over his bare brown arms and fastened his unbuttoned cuffs.

'I mistook you for someone else, I'm sorry. It was arranged that I should meet the property agent here. Do you know where I can find her?' he asked in his softly accented English.

'She's probably at home by now, having dealt with

at least two more clients in the time it took you to get here,' Kira snapped, still unsettled by the unexpected embrace. Stefano's face remained expressionless, but his eyes glittered, and suddenly Kira regretted her rudeness to this rather formidable man. Then his mouth curled with sudden humour.

'Dio—it's been a long time since anyone spoke to me like that!'

In that puzzled instant, years fell away from his face and he looked much younger. Kira was momentarily thrown off balance. His beautiful eyes and quizzical expression were almost too much to bear. She had to swallow hard before she spoke again, but she'd be damned if she'd let him walk all over her just because she couldn't stop staring at his mouth.

'I'm sorry, *signore*, but you have turned up over three hours late—without any apology—and flown ridiculously low over this valley, terrifying the wildlife and ruining a beautiful evening,' she said firmly, quailing slightly inside as his expression turned stormy. Someone like this didn't hear enough straight talking in his working life. He had just said as much himself.

'If I have caused offence, I apologise,' he said, slightly stiffly. 'Not having the neighbours flying in overhead all the time is a big selling point as far as I am concerned.' Then his features softened. 'I am Stefano Albani, by the way. I'm interested in buying the Bella Terra estate. That's why I assumed you were Miss Barrett, the agent. I thought you were welcoming me with cries of delight!' he joked, searching her expression as he spoke, his mocking eyes somehow piercing her outraged manner and making it irritatingly difficult to stay angry.

'Well, I wasn't,' Kira said, biting back everything

else she felt like telling him. She had to tread carefully. Stefano Albani might have arrived late and lascivious, but there was, unfortunately, a chance he would become her new neighbour and there was no point in making it more difficult than it had to be.

Stefano compressed his lips at the note of accusation in her voice.

He has a really beautiful mouth, Kira caught herself thinking, before his frown dragged her attention back to the Mediterranean depths of his eyes.

'A delay put me behind schedule, and I wanted to get here as fast as I could. That meant flying. Besides, the disturbance was over in a few seconds. I'm sure the valley has recovered from much worse over the years. People always try to imprint themselves on the countryside. The land shakes them all off, sooner or later.'

Kira's alarm must have shown in her face. He quickly softened his tone and added, 'You have my promise that it won't happen again. There will be no low flying in this valley after I move in.'

His words were quite definite, but the essence of a smile still hovered around his lips. When he looked like that, it was impossible for Kira to look away. There was plenty to see. With the air cleared between them, his eyes were now the untroubled blue of a perfect Italian sky. His dark hair was a riot of soft curls, short enough to be neat but long enough to move slightly in the warm air rising from the parched earth at their feet. He was undoubtedly powerful, but it was the strength of steel hawsers rather than unsophisticated animal bulk. Unlike the millionaires Kira had worked for in the past, this man looked as though he used his body as hard as his brain. She could never imagine him parked behind a computer console. She wished she had paid more attention when Amanda Barrett had been rabbiting on about the wonderful Signor Albani. At the time, Kira had shut her ears. Thank goodness the estate agent wasn't here now. She would have fallen for this man like a lead weight.

It's all too easy to see how women must do that, Kira thought darkly. With bewildered fascination, she wondered why they didn't see him for what he must really be—a rich pleasure seeker with no thought for anyone but himself. She could tell exactly the sort of man he was, simply by the way he brimmed with self-assurance. Kira watched him looking up at the grand old building as though he already owned it. She tried to ignore a shiver of apprehension, and told herself looks meant nothing. He hadn't stepped over the villa's threshold yet. How could he be so sure this was the place for him?

'We'll see—if you move in,' she replied grimly, wondering if she held any influence over his purchase. Maybe it's time to forget what I think about Stefano Albani, and start wondering what he might be thinking about me, Kira told herself. Stefano seemed like the kind of man who might actually thrive on opposition rather than avoid it. She decided to try and muffle her objections, for as long as it took this man to make up his mind about the villa and estate. She told herself sharply that this had nothing to do with not wanting to appear like an angry shrew in front of such a gorgeous man.

'The fact is, *signore*, I was only waiting here with the estate details and keys, because I was confident you would never turn up,' she told him. 'I had my whole evening planned until you dropped out of the sky—'

'And wrecked all your plans?'

Kira's scowl returned. 'I was going to say you gave me the fright of my life and apologise for the way I reacted,' she replied frostily.

Stefano said nothing. Instead, he reached out his hand. Kira stared woodenly at his smooth, pale palm until she realised what he was after. She pushed the property details at him. They had been turned around in her nervous hands for too long, and he had to smooth out some creases before he could begin to read.

'What did I stop you doing this evening?' he asked after a few moments' study. His eyes never left the printed page, so the question caught Kira off guard.

'Nothing, as usual,' she replied instantly, before re-membering what she had said to him in the heat of her anger.

He looked up from the brochure with a smile that glittered like pearl against his golden skin.

'In that case, why don't you show me around this old place?'

The offer was so unexpected, Kira replied without thinking. 'Oh, I'd love to!'

She regretted the words in an instant. This wasn't her job. She had no business here. She had simply of-fered to hand over the details and keys, before disap-pearing. That was the deal—nothing more. She tried to backtrack. 'Yes, I'd love to, Signor Albani, although I'm only a neighbour.' She looked up at the lovely old house and heaved a long, heartfelt sigh. 'I don't really know anything about the place. I've only seen inside one or two rooms before—'

'"It has been owned by an Englishman for many years,"' Stefano read aloud from the notes. 'Do you know him?'

'Sir Ivan was my client. I was his landscape consultant. That's all,' she added hurriedly.

'I suppose you two English people both "kept yourselves to yourselves," in that well-worn phrase?' Stefano's wry smile made Kira feel defensive. However right he may be, she didn't like that he assumed so much about her. Piqued, she ignored her impulse to refuse him.

'I'll gladly show you around outside, *signore*. There's no one who knows more than I do about the estate and the gardens here, but you'll be better off with the brochure when it comes to viewing the house.'

'You're a landscape consultant, you say?' His smile dimmed as he looked her over with a different intensity. Kira reddened as he studied her working clothes of dusty jeans and simple white shirt. Seeing her reaction, his generous mouth lifted in a grin.

'But why are we wasting time out here talking, when we could be looking around this beautiful house? If I know English women—which I do,' he said in a way that needed absolutely no explanation, 'I'm sure you are as keen as I am to get inside the villa and have a good look around. So come with me now. What do you say?'

There was nothing Kira could say. He was talking about a tour of the house she had spent two years dreaming and wondering about. She had been trying to pluck up the nerve to have a peek inside before he arrived, but couldn't bring herself to do it. Now he was inviting her in....

Without waiting for her answer, he started forward. Holding the Bella Terra brochure in one hand, he touched her waist lightly with the other. Kira found herself drawn gently towards the big old building. His pat of encouragement was enjoyable in a way she did not want it to be. Putting on a little more speed, she moved fractionally ahead of his hand. She reached the steps of the house just in front of him. Then there was a pause as Stefano used the great iron key to unlock the door. Standing aside, he let Kira enter first. Still she hesitated. She was desperate to poke around the villa, but on her own. Quite apart from him possibly becoming the villa's next owner, exploring such a beautiful place with Stefano Albani felt somehow much too intimate.

Stefano had none of her misgivings. His hand connected with her waist again, gently urging her to enter. A little sigh left Kira's lips. It felt dangerously like the sound of her scorn softening around the edges. He stayed where he was, but inclined his head politely. 'After you. I need to see everything, so I'm afraid this may take some time.'

He spoke softly, but with absolute authority. He was acting as though the house already belonged to him. Kira coloured guiltily. She had enjoyed the run of this valley for so long she considered it to be her own private haven. Now she finally had a chance to look around the villa at its heart, but the company of such a man added an extra frisson of excitement. If she was honest, it was the surprising intensity of this feeling which was making her hesitate.

What if she couldn't think of enough to say? She had got out of the habit of small talk. Flustered, she looked around wildly for help. Why, she had no idea. There was no one for miles. She had never felt so alone. This man scrambled her brains. He had totally blown away all her common sense. She looked into his eyes and saw things she recognised from the reflection in her bathroom mirror each morning. His blue eyes spoke words that never reached his lips, and she knew that look. Aside from his dangerously smooth assurance, there might be a deeper, darker reason to beware. He might have secrets like hers hiding beneath that sophisticated surface. Unaccountably, she felt the need to peel away his seductive veneer and find out the truth beneath the image.

The weight of Stefano's hand began to rest against her a little more noticeably. At first it had been the merest brush of his fingertips. Now his palm settled gently in the hollow of her back, like falling snow.

With terrifying clarity, Kira imagined it sliding around to encircle her waist again. It felt so good, it had to be wrong. Swallowing hard, she suppressed every wild, unfamiliar instinct and announced quietly, 'Please don't touch me, Signor Albani.'

His hand fell away. He stepped back, surprised.

'Are you sure?'

'I'm positive.'

He stared at her, trying to puzzle out her expression. Kira willed herself to return his look blandly.

'That's interesting,' he murmured at length.

After studying her face, he let his gaze drift at leisure over her body.

'First you answer me back, but now you're as nervous as a kitten,' he mused, his eyes hooded with thought. 'I came to look at property. It seems that's not the only thing around here that might be worth investigating.'

CHAPTER TWO

'DON'T flatter me, or yourself,' Kira muttered, beginning to fuss with the belt of her jeans. It felt wrong to be exploring such a place in her dusty work clothes; somehow she felt that the villa demanded a sense of occasion. He was standing so close to her that the temptation to study him was next to irresistible. Instead, she concentrated on brushing herself down, removing any stray grass seeds before she crossed the threshold of the grand house.

'Don't worry. It's a villa, not the Vatican!' He chuckled, again exhibiting a disquieting ability to read her thoughts. 'You look fine. You're one of those women who look good in anything.'

Kira glanced up sharply at his unexpected compliment. He laughed as their gazes connected. She couldn't stop staring at him, and when he caught her eye it sent a confusion of signals through her body.

'You're right. I'm only looking around a house, that's all. It's nothing more than that,' Kira murmured, trying to stake her claim to innocence. This Stefano Albani was strangely magnetic. Leaving him to investigate on his own might mean she never saw him again. If she followed him, she would delay the moment of parting and get to view the property of her dreams, too.

'So if you are ready, *signore*, shall we make a start?' she added with a bit more confidence.

He laughed again. 'Suddenly so businesslike! I'm making the effort to leave the world behind for a while. Why don't you do the same? I suspect it would do us both good to live a little, for once.' His gaze was uncomfortably direct and Kira shifted under it. 'In fact, it occurs to me that I don't even know your name. So, as we begin, why don't we start with some simple introductions? You know who I am, but who are you?'

Kira had often wondered that herself. 'That isn't important, Signor Albani.' She shook her shoulders irritably.

'Of course it is!'

'No, really. I'm nobody.'

'Don't be ridiculous.' His smile showed signs of fading. 'Everybody is somebody. Your name is your own. You can give it to me.'

Kira stopped. Ignoring this danger sign, Stefano didn't.

'Go on. You know you want to, and it won't hurt!' he teased her gently.

His question revived all Kira's pain. The isolation of Bella Terra meant she didn't have to introduce herself more than once or twice a year. That suited her. Every time she spoke her name, it reminded her of the shame she had left behind in England.

'It's Kira Banks,' she muttered. Head down, she tried to cross the threshold but Stefano blocked her retreat.

'You don't sound very happy about it.' His air

was light, but she saw interrogation in his relentless blue gaze.

Blast him, what was wrong with the man? Kira was used to people backing off, becoming bored when met with her reluctance to talk about herself. In her experience most people preferred to be talking about themselves in any case. It appeared Signor Albani was used to having his questions answered.

'Why is that?' Stefano persisted quietly in the face of her continued silence.

Kira wanted to stare him out but her features lost the struggle. They were moving of their own accord. Her lids would not obey. She lowered her lashes, unable to struggle against the depth of his gaze. Making up some excuse for any other person would have been easy enough, but Stefano Albani was looking down at her with a fiction-piercing stare that demanded nothing less than the truth.

She gritted her teeth and muttered, 'I came here to escape. I wanted to live in a place where no one knows my name.'

He drew back from her a little.

'Okay, I'll let it go at that…' he relented, although his face told a different story. 'For now…' he added with a smile.

Kira mastered her features and managed a bland smile.

'Don't say I have stumbled on a master criminal, living in her bolthole in Italy?'

He was teasing her again. She managed to lift her eyes to challenge him, but knew she couldn't afford to rise to his bait. Her pain hovered too close to the surface.

She didn't need him to aggravate her injuries. There were other people only too willing to do that.

'Why I'm here is nobody's business but my own.' She tried not to snap, but it was difficult. Only his steady gaze softened her reaction. 'In any case, the reasons would take far too long to explain, Signor Albani. Some things are best kept private. Why don't we stop wasting time, and start looking around this lovely house?'

Purposely keeping her voice casual, she jerked herself out of his grasp. She could not escape his expression so easily. It was like a caress. It took all her determination to break eye contact with him. She managed it by concentrating on the breathtaking photograph on the cover of the property brochure in his hand. It was the only sure way she could distract herself from the delicious dangers of this man. Stefano gestured for her to walk across the entrance hall first. It was large, cool, and it echoed with his slow footsteps as he followed her across the cracked marble tiles.

Kira took a good look around. She had only ever entered the villa by one of the back doors. This was her first time in the grand public areas, and she didn't want to miss a thing. While she was daydreaming, Stefano strolled past her. Pulling a pearl-handled penknife from his pocket, he pushed the blade against the woodwork of the nearest door. Kira gazed in wonder at the ornate plasterwork, and the beautifully worked banisters on the great double staircase, but he was busy with more practical things. He worked his way methodically around the entrance hall, testing, checking and inspecting.

'This is the most beautiful house I have ever seen,' she said wistfully. Stefano was not so easily impressed.

'My town house in Florence is more practical, and in

better condition,' he observed, before flashing another brilliant smile at her. 'But you're right. The setting and space here can't be beaten.'

Kira nodded. 'It's a lovely house. Oh, yes, there are bound to be things about it that must be altered, updated or replaced. It's old. But I'd like nothing better than the chance to give it some homely touches. Couldn't you just imagine the scene in December, with a fifteen-foot Christmas tree standing in that bay between the staircases?'

Stefano looked over to where she pointed. He studied the space, tipping his head first one way, and then the other.

'Yes, the proportions would be exactly right. That's important with these old houses. Everything must be in scale,' he said firmly.

Kira's heart gave a strange flutter. She had been half joking, hardly expecting the big-shot billionaire to consider Christmas trees with such seriousness. That might be a glimmer of hope. Even if he might fill the place with rowdy celebrity friends, he clearly had an eye for the important things in life.

'A tree like that in a place like this will need to hit exactly the right note. When I host my first Christmas party I want everyone to be speechless with delight— because I'm all for a quiet life.' He smiled, and gave her a look of undisguised interest. 'So that's the festive season sorted out. What do you suggest for my house-warming extravaganza?'

It was a totally unexpected question. Kira looked to see if he was trying to wind her up. He gazed back innocently. Smiling in spite of herself, she decided to answer in the same spirit.

'Actually, I'm the last person you should ask about entertaining. I'm a garden designer. I prefer to work with plants rather than people.'

'What is a Christmas tree, if it isn't a plant?' He shrugged. 'And I shall need all sorts of those. When we become neighbours I shall want your advice, sooner or later.'

Kira shot him a look of pure disbelief. 'You can have exactly what you like, *signore*. You don't need anyone to advise you, let alone me!'

'There are times when everyone can do with a little help,' he slung straight back at her. 'By employing skilled people, I can spend my time and effort on all the things I really want to do. In this instance, it gives me plenty of time to plan for Christmas.' He stopped inspecting the paintwork and turned an acute gaze on her. 'I know— you must have a good eye for colour. How would you like the task of co-ordinating all the decorations?'

Kira nearly laughed out loud. It felt truly bizarre to be standing in a vast Tuscan villa in the heat of summer, talking about something that was months away.

'Why on earth would you want someone else to decorate your Christmas tree? It's something I've looked forward to every year for as long as I can remember! It's the chance to be a child again, I suppose, without all the pressure.'

It was Stefano's turn to look askance. 'I know all about pressure.' His voice darkened with meaning.

Kira groaned under the weight of memory. 'That's why it's so good to get away from it all, to a place like this. I can enjoy Christmas my way. No rehearsing recitals in Gloucester cathedral, dashing between carol services and amateur dramatics, torturing tons of holly, ivy and mistletoe into wreaths and swags. When I was a child, it was never ending.'

He pursed his lips, and then said drily, 'It's a wonder you had any time to yourself.'

'I didn't. That's the penalty you pay for being a trophy child, isn't it?'

'I wouldn't know. I missed out on all that. I skipped it, and went straight from sleeping in a box under the table, to earning a living.'

'Gosh, you must have had a deprived childhood!' she joked.

He stared at her, unimpressed. His eyes were suddenly chill with all the hidden feelings she recognised from her own reflection. She stopped laughing.

'Yes. Yes, I did.' He grazed his lower lip with his teeth for a moment, and then added, 'But that's behind me now. The future is all that matters.'

There was iron-hard determination in his voice. His eyes were everywhere. She wondered what havoc he would wreak on this beautiful old house when he took possession of it. The thought worried her. A few moments ago, she had been annoyed by the way he talked as though the villa was already his. Now she was thinking about it in the same way. He was checking every inch of the building like the rightful owner. If ever a man was made to lord it over the Bella Terra valley, it's Stefano Albani, she thought, with a shiver of apprehension.

'You're cold. Why don't you step outside into the evening sun and warm up?' he murmured.

His words surprised her. She thought all his attention was riveted on the villa's sales brochure, and hadn't expected him to notice.

'No, I'm fine,' she said quickly, unwilling to miss this

chance to look over the grand villa she gazed at every day from her favourite viewpoint on the other side of the valley.

His eyes glittered with sudden fire. 'As long as you're sure.'

Kira began to feel uneasy. Every time he looked at her, he smiled as he spoke. It was an unusual expression, caressing the most secret parts of her. As she tried not to shrink beneath his gaze, she felt the peaks of her nipples push against the smooth profile of her thin shirt. They stiffened still more to know he was looking at her. It was no longer the chill of the cool marble hall affecting her body. He must have realised it, too, but looked away sharply as obvious appreciation flared for a moment in his eyes.

Kira didn't know what to do. Putting her head down, she scuttled off towards the nearest door.

'Let's see what's through here, shall we?' she said, bursting into the first room beyond the entrance hall. Within half a step she stopped. It was the reception room that time forgot. Sunlight streamed through tall, graceful windows but its beams danced with dust motes. The design of the room was in a typically grand Italian style, although its furnishings wouldn't have been out of place in an English country house.

'Oh, my goodness!' Kira exclaimed. 'A little bit of England overseas!'

Following close behind her, Stefano clicked his tongue when he saw her shudder.

'My stepparents have spent a lifetime collecting stuff like this. Cane-back chairs, chintz upholstery and Goss china. Sir Ivan must have shipped everything over here from England. Why on earth would you move to Italy, then recreate England in your new home?'

'I don't know.' Stefano was equally put out at the sight. His mouth was a stern line of disapproval. 'Some foreigners buy up these properties claiming to love Italy. In reality, Toscana is nothing more to them than England with better weather. They are more interested in worshipping their own land from a safe distance.'

'I'm not. I love it here,' Kira told him. 'I couldn't wait to leave England behind, decorations and all...' She paused, wondering whether to push her luck, and decided she had nothing to lose.

'If we're going to be neighbours, I'd feel happier if I knew you were going to treat this old place well,' she went on. 'It would be such a shame to see it spoilt.'

'It won't matter to you for a few weeks a year, surely?' He shrugged.

Kira was puzzled. 'So you're going to be away a lot?'

'No, but you'll be leaving with the summer, won't you?'

Kira coloured up angrily. 'Why should I?'

'So you won't be flitting between here and your home in England?' He looked surprised.

She shook her head defiantly. 'No! I thought I'd made it clear—I don't have a home in England any more. In any case, I couldn't bear to leave at the end of summer, as the holiday-home owners do. How could I abandon my home here? The Bella Terra valley is everything I want—peace and beauty.'

Stefano's dark brows lightened a little. 'I assume that means you could find no peace in England, so you brought your beauty here?'

His voice was low and melodious but his eyes shone with mischief. Drawn to look straight at him again, Kira could not help lifting her lips in the ghost of a smile, but she said nothing.

'I don't know of many people who would willingly hide away in such an isolated spot,' he murmured. 'You're not afraid to stand up for yourself, you work for your living and you love this place as much as I intend to. How could anything make such a forthright, independent woman leave England under a cloud?'

Kira lifted one hand and began to fiddle with a skein of her dark auburn hair.

'It was a combination of things,' she said, hoping to stop him asking any more awkward questions.

He lifted his brows still higher, encouraging her to unburden herself. She shifted from foot to foot. Her fingers moved from her hair to toy with the thin gold chain around her neck. Stefano watched her. He seemed genuinely interested, and ready to listen. Suddenly she was tired of bottling everything up, and keeping herself to herself. She wanted to talk. She needed someone who might sympathise, or at least answer back. It hardly mattered about the words. She had never seen Stefano Albani before today, and might never see him again. He had already proved himself to be sympathetic. If she explained the whole miserable business to him, as an impartial third party, it might make her feel better.

It was on the tip of her tongue to tell him the whole sorry story. She pushed the guilty words against her teeth, trying to force them out. It was no good. She had kept silent for so long, she didn't know where to begin. Finally, she shook her head.

'It's nothing.'

He considered her gravely. 'I think it is. Something is obviously weighing heavily on your mind.'

He took a step towards her. Kira knew he moved almost silently, but the brush of his leather-soled shoes sounded loud in the peace of the reception room. She stared at the floor. She winced when his feet appeared in her field of view, but it was still a shock to feel the gentle touch of his hand on her shoulder.

'There's no need to jump. I'm only offering a little support,' he said.

'I don't need it,' she said staunchly, but he took no notice and never moved. His touch was warm, reassuring...seductive. In spite of herself, Kira relished the feeling. Then he spoiled the effect. His touch vibrated slightly. She looked up, and saw laughter in his eyes.

'One day, I would really enjoy the chance to discuss sins with you, Miss Kira Banks. Whatever you may have done, I'm sure I can top it!'

With a sharp twist of her head, Kira looked away. She could not bear to let him see her misery. Squeezing her lids tightly closed, she battled to stop the tears falling. She was so lost in her own despair she was completely unprepared for what happened next. Stefano closed the gap between them. His arms glided around her. She was drawn into his body again, and it felt so natural she. let it happen without a word. For a few heart-stopping seconds she leaned against him. The sensation of his shirt pressed against her cheek and the enveloping male fragrance of him closed her eyes.

'Is there anything I can do?' His voice echoed around the unloved caverns of the villa.

Kira shook her head. 'I'd be grateful if you could

just drop the subject,' she managed, with a trace of steel showing through her muttered words.

'Okay.'

He took his time in releasing her. Kira normally disliked physical contact, but this was different. Stefano seemed to specialise in the sort of touch she might like to experience again.

He obviously wasn't going to give up on her. Kira sensed he couldn't resist a challenge any more than she could. However, she also knew her fragile self-esteem couldn't stand too many questions. Her reaction to unwarranted attention was usually to snap first, and apologise later. It appeared that this hadn't dissuaded Stefano in the slightest. The most disconcerting thing about that was how ready she'd been to indulge in the comfort he offered. *Pull yourself together!* she ordered herself silently. This man was clearly used to getting his own way and she was embarrassed how easily she had mistaken his charm for anything more permanent.

A hint of her old defiance returned. It allowed her to face him calmly, but it didn't stop her cheeks flaming red at how much she had nearly revealed. 'I'm sorry, *signore*. That was a momentary lapse, but now you'll see that I really don't want to talk about it. So I'd be grateful if we could leave it at that. Okay?' she finished crisply.

Stefano's gaze ebbed away from her as she spoke. He said nothing. Instead, he tightened his lips, and bobbed his head once in silent agreement. In the pause that followed, he glanced around. His eyes, like his body, were restless.

'Everyone has parts of their lives they're not proud

of,' he conceded. 'I can relate to that. So if we agree on a truce, can we continue with the tour?'

He had been almost teasing as he tried to extract her secret, but now he had retreated again behind that impenetrable mask. Kira felt a strange pang of loss. She wondered if he ever experienced the sort of social unease that tortured her. It seemed unlikely. What could ever make such a man feel inadequate?

She nodded and gave him a fleeting smile. 'Of course.'

What would it feel like to unburden herself to him? She was certain he would listen. Really listen, and not simply humour her because he wanted something. Life would take on a different dimension. It was something she had never bothered about before, but a few seconds in Stefano's arms had opened up a whole new world of possibilities for her. It almost tempted her out of her shell, but not quite. If he couldn't be on time for a business appointment, he was hardly likely to treat a casual acquaintance any better. She gave up on the idea. At least when she was on the defensive, she couldn't be hurt.

'If you are really interested in buying the Bella Terra estate, Signor Albani, you should be making the most of your visit. You mustn't stand around here with me.'

Without waiting for his reply, she turned her back on him and walked out of the sunlit room. The vast, gloomy hall beyond was supposed to cool her feelings.

'There's no need to run away from me, Kira.'

She stopped.

'You might be surprised,' she said finally.

Her darkening attitude didn't bother Stefano at all.

He stuck one hand casually in his pocket, and grinned at her.

'So what are you waiting for, then? Surprise me.'

His words made her uncertain. Until a short time ago, endless surprises—none of them good—had been the story of her life. Then she had escaped, and moved to Italy. For a couple of years she had experienced wonderful freedom. And now, with the loss of Sir Ivan, her foremost client, she was faced with the threat that happiness might soon be snatched away from her again. Unconsciously, her shoulders began to sag. Then she sensed his gaze was still on her. She looked up. He was still quizzing her with his eyes.

She shrugged. 'I'm afraid there's nothing more to me than you see here, *signore*.'

His face was totally impassive but he went on watching her as he said quietly, 'Then it's a good job I came here to see the Bella Terra estate, rather than anything else. My journey won't have been entirely wasted,' he announced before setting off across the hall again. 'Now, down to business. I want to look around this house. Would you like to come with me?'

CHAPTER THREE

TOGETHER, they began to walk.

'Why did Bella Terra's owner—the English gentle-man—leave you alone here?' Stefano was looking at her in a new way. Kira preferred the old one, but still felt her cheeks flare.

'He died.'

For the first time, the smile left Stefano's eyes. 'Then I'm sorry.'

His sympathy looked genuine. Kira decided to give him the benefit of the doubt. 'He was eighty-five, *signore*, so it was hardly unexpected.'

He shrugged. 'But it must have been a shock, all the same. Deaths are always tragic.' His last words grated uncomfortably in the marble-lined hall. Kira recognised a dangerous flash in his eyes. She couldn't help noticing the length and thickness of his soot-dark lashes. *He* probably knows they are one of his best features, she warned herself abruptly. It can be the only reason he keeps looking at me like that.

'I'm sorry you lost a friend, Kira. I know what that is like.' His voice was distant and regretful. Something about the tone hinted that he had his own secrets.

He shook his head suddenly, as if discarding old

memories and turned to her, a playful smile again curving the corners of his mouth, taking refuge in flirtation.

'Kira—that is a beautiful name for a lovely woman. Coupled with your shining auburn hair, jade-green eyes and magnolia skin, what more could any man want?'

That broke the spell.

'Nothing—until his wife finds out.' Sidestepping him smartly, Kira headed back across the shady hall towards the only parts of the house she had seen before. That way she could put a little distance between them, without losing contact entirely. People made her uneasy, and that feeling fed on itself. Every time she began to warm towards Stefano, she felt bound to pull herself back into line. Yet increasingly, his every move held her hypnotised. When he started sweet talking her, it was too tender a reminder of how things could turn sour all too soon.

'I have no worries on that score, Kira. I don't have a wife.'

She heard his footsteps fall in beside her, but did not look at him.

'That's what they all say—to begin with, Signor Albani.'

'Call me Stefano.'

'They all say that, too.'

Walking over to the glazed door at the rear of the building, she unlocked it. When open, it would give him a view into the courtyard garden beyond. The fresh air and perfume of flowers always soothed her. Kira had designed this entire quadrangle garden. Originally, it was nothing more than cracked concrete and stagnant slime. Now it was one of her triumphs. Stefano was sure to be distracted once he got out there. She was looking forward to seeing what he thought of her work. It would be good to get an unbiased opinion. She knew that would help take her mind off her troubles, more than anything else.

It had always been a struggle to free the warped woodwork of the garden door. Although the interior paintwork was smart brown gloss, Kira knew it was a different story on the other side. The Tuscan sun had roasted away the shine within months. Now sunburnt flakes speckled the steps and sills. She tugged at the door, but it was only when Stefano came to help that it could finally be dragged back over the uneven tiles.

The large rectangular courtyard was paved with local cream-coloured stone. Around its boundary ran a deep, shady colonnade. In the centre was a raised fish pool. The air beyond the hall was still and hot. It hung over the threshold like a heavy curtain. Kira stepped outside, and Stefano followed her into the stormy sunshine. His hair glittered like jet as he looked around the garden. A large ceanothus had been planted in one corner. It hummed with bees, their sound joining the quiet splash of water trickling over wet stones. Ornamental ferns grew in the shadiest areas. The ones with smooth, satiny leaves enjoyed the damp soil and mosses in deepest shadow. Those with leaflets like lace rippled in the slightest breeze, patterning the old riven flagstones with light and shade. The coping stones around the pool were wide and warm. Stefano strolled over, and sat down. Leaning on one hand, he looked into the water.

'This is spectacular. Come and join me,' he drawled, his voice languorous in the heat.

Kira took her time. She didn't want to seem too eager;

being close to him seemed to rob her of her usual self-composure. She walked over and perched on the opposite side of the pool.

'I love this place already. What a beautiful oasis!' For the first time since she'd met him, Stefano seemed to relax completely, breathing in the fragrant air and gazing around with unaffected pleasure.

'Thank you. I wanted to give old Sir Ivan somewhere on the ground floor that he could enjoy, whatever the weather.'

'You are responsible for this?' His brows lifted appreciatively.

'Yes—and all the other recent work you'll see when you inspect the grounds. Sir Ivan saw one of my garden designs on display at the Chelsea Flower Show, several years ago. He commissioned me to create a roof garden for his town house in London. After that, I did more and more projects for him and his friends, before relocating here permanently two years ago.'

Stefano's beautiful mouth twitched in appreciation. 'So you're a self-made woman? Congratulations.'

'I'm only doing my job.' Kira shrugged.

'Don't be so modest! Word of mouth may have brought you a long way in business so far, but with the death of your friend Sir Ivan, you must have lost a major client. You'll need to find a replacement. Have you got anyone lined up?' he asked suddenly.

Kira shook her head. She had been trying not to think about that. She really hated having to publicise her business. The more people who contacted her because they had seen and enjoyed her work through their friends, the better.

'If I'm honest, all I enjoy is the work. Dealing with people is a nightmare I wish I could avoid for ever.'

Stefano cleared his throat. Kira wondered if he was as surprised as she was by how honest she was being with him. At least he liked her garden, which was a good sign. Standing, she brushed off her memories of working in this peaceful sanctuary. Once Stefano Albani came to live here, she might never see inside this place again. She ought to make the most of this tour.

It was a poignant moment. As Stefano stepped out of the stark sunlight and back into the shadows, Kira hesitated. The shade should have been a wonderful relief from the hot afternoon. Instead, she felt the chill of abandonment, and not for the first time. It was the story of her life. She had been given up as a lost cause by her stepparents. Then her place on the sidelines of their life became permanent when their unexpected natural child arrived. Now she was doing much the same to the garden she had cherished. In a few weeks or months, she would have to turn her back on this place and leave it in the hands of others. She shuddered.

Stefano noticed, and smiled at her in a way calculated to immediately warm her up.

'It sounds as though you will be my perfect neighbour.'

Kira shot him a look that said she didn't share his view.

'I promise the experience will be an unforgettable one,' he added quietly.

She ignored that, and told him the simple truth. 'I'm afraid anyone who buys this house automatically gets on the wrong side of me. Sir Ivan and I used to co-exist in this valley very well. I can't imagine anyone else being a better neighbour than he was.'

She thought it would be safer to warn Stefano what she was like, right from the beginning. Instead of sympathising, he laughed.

'I'll try,' he said mischievously. 'Let's hope I can play the part as well as you act the role of estate agent!'

His refusal to take her statement seriously was infuriating. 'I'm not acting. I'm here to make sure nothing happens to the villa keys,' she said stiffly. 'You're here to view the place. We've got nothing in common, and we're never going to see each other again after today.'

Stefano said nothing, but smiled at her with an assessing look in his meltingly dark eyes. The dappled sunshine played on his clean, beautiful features and suddenly the thought of never seeing him again wasn't quite as comforting as she had expected.

As they continued their tour of the house, Kira began to wonder if she had misjudged the captivating Signor Stefano Albani. They did have one thing in common. It was obvious the moment they reached the first floor. He strode straight to the nearest window and looked out. Only when he had inspected the vista with its avenue of sweetly scented lime trees did he begin his careful study of the floors, walls and furnishings. Watching him, she noticed he carried out the same ritual with each new room they entered. He paid no attention to the high ceilings and airily beautiful rooms until he had studied what was on show outside. Finally, she couldn't stay silent any longer.

'I see you like the view,' she said with satisfaction.

There was a pause before he answered. It gave her

strange pleasure to see that he carried on drinking in the scenery before he replied. 'Is it so obvious?'

'You make a beeline for the windows each time we enter a room.'

He frowned, seeming uncomfortable that she had noticed his simple enjoyment of their beautiful surroundings.

'I'm simply checking to see where the nearest neighbours are. I value my privacy.'

Kira nodded, covering a smile. 'I understand. This valley is perfect for that. You won't be disturbed. Let's hope you don't disturb me!'

He gave her a sharp look, then paced on towards the next room. As he walked, he compared what he was seeing with the beautifully produced brochure. Kira decided to get a copy of the booklet for herself. It would be a permanent reminder of this day, and the house. She was seeing it for the first and last time, and that made her happy to wander along in Stefano's wake. He needed no commentary, and took his time. While he judged and estimated distances and sizes, Kira simply enjoyed herself. The old house was beautiful. Its corridors and great rooms had a quiet grace, despite all the grime and dust. Sir Ivan couldn't have visited the upper storeys of his house in years. There were worm-eaten long-case clocks on plinths, dusty carriage clocks on equally dusty coffee tables and delicate little china clocks on every mantelpiece. There wasn't so much as a tick or a tock between them. All were silent. All were sad. Only the sound of a golden oriole warbling from the lime trees outside and swifts screaming overhead broke the thick summer silence.

'Ah, perfetto,' Stefano breathed, with a look of total

satisfaction. Kira was entranced. As he strolled on into the final room on the top floor, she stopped. There was no point in going any further. The small, square box room was no competition for her last uninterrupted viewing of Stefano Albani. She watched as he finished inspecting the house that might become his own. He moved with the self-assured grace of a man who would be at home anywhere. His gestures were expansive as he waved the brochure in her direction, drawing her attention to some fact or another. He only became still when he returned to his favourite position, at the window. Kira felt somehow relieved to see him at rest, if only for a short while. He gave the impression of continuous movement, no matter how slight. She found that unsettling. When he was still like this, lost in thought, she could almost imagine he was at peace. Almost…but not quite. There was always a trace of tension lingering around those eyes. When he forgot to try and charm her, they held the thousand-mile stare of a troubled man.

She found herself drawn inexorably towards him. Silently, she moved across the bare floorboards, past anonymous, dust-sheeted furniture. The need to reach out and touch him again before he was lost to her forever was irresistible.

And then he moved. The moment was broken. He turned to her in surprise, but then a slow smile warmed his features, and she realised she had raised a hand as though to touch him.

'Go ahead. Be my guest. As we're going to be neighbours, it's a good idea for us to get to know each other better, wouldn't you say?'

Kira pulled her hand back as though she had been burned. 'I—I was going to brush a cobweb from your shoulder. You know how dusty these old houses can be…' She faltered, convincing neither of them.

Stefano was intrigued. Kira was full of contradictions. Half of her seemed to be yearning towards him, but something kept pulling her back. With another woman, he might have taken advantage of the situation straight away, but he wasn't about to push his luck with Miss Kira Banks—not for a while, at least. She interested him.

In the short time they had been together, he recognised the pain in her. It was too close to home. He wondered how deep the similarities ran between him and this privileged young Englishwoman. Once, when he was young, he had come face to face with tragedy. He could have let it crush him to powder. He dodged that, but paid a heavy price. From that moment, he had spent his whole life on the run. He was afraid of nothing but his conscience. This woman didn't need to draw pictures when she spoke to him. She had escaped from somewhere and ended up here. That was enough information for him—for the moment. He knew what it felt like to be goaded by guilt.

The fact we've both decided on this hidden valley is somehow comforting, he thought, and then cursed sharply. What did he need with comfort? All he wanted was somewhere he could withdraw from his hectic business life and enjoy some quality time. The Bella Terra estate offered everything he wanted. And it had the added advantage that at least one of the neighbours shared his love of solitude.

* * *

'I really enjoyed that,' Kira said as they reached the front doors again after the grand tour.

'You sound surprised?' He raised his eyebrows.

'I am! I only agreed to stand in for that estate agent because I was sure you wouldn't turn up this afternoon. I tend to try and avoid people, when I can.'

'You couldn't avoid me,' Stefano reminded her, stepping out of the house and striding off across the terrace. He was intent on seeing the grounds. That made Kira nervous. The bulky clouds rising up over the far ridge of hills were backlit by a blood-red sun. Despite that warning, he kept heading away from his helicopter, and towards the storm. Kira didn't share his confidence.

'Shouldn't you be going, Stefano?' she called, needing to draw his attention to the threatening sky.

He turned. 'Anyone would think you were trying to get rid of me! I like this place, Kira. I want to see the rest of it.'

'But it's going to rain!'

He was unimpressed. 'Get wet, get dry again. That's my motto. I'm going to be living in this beautiful villa, so I should start thinking like a country person. Maybe I can learn to look on the trees as nature's umbrella.'

Kira wasn't sure if he was joking. She hated uncertainty, and followed him to find out. A growl of thunder prowled into the valley, which was something else she didn't like. She stopped dead.

'You're going to walk around the grounds in this weather? You might get struck by lightning! Are you mad?'

He paused. 'I've been called many things in my time, but never that!' After another second's thought, he started towards her as rapidly as the storm. As he reached her side, he narrowed his eyes. 'Are you scared? Is that it?'

'Of course not,' Kira said, raising her chin defiantly and determined to shadow him whatever the weather might throw at them. 'Nothing scares me.'

He didn't look convinced, but swung away across the terrace again.

'Come on, then. I've seen enough of your landscape work from the upper floors to know that I want you to work for me,' he announced, leaving her to run and catch him up. 'After hearing about what you did for Sir Ivan, I've decided my town house in Florence needs a new designer. I want more greenery, and a roof garden. When you're not busy with that, you can act as consultant to some inner-city work I'm funding. Currently, it lacks focus. Community projects have been successful elsewhere. Your input may be exactly what I need. I'll want you to design something to appeal to everyone, and then organise working parties to—'

'Wait!' Kira tried to halt the imperious flow of instructions. 'That all sounds good and important, but I can't simply drop everything on your say-so!'

He stopped, as the sun went behind a cloud.

'Why not?' He stared at her, uncomprehending.

'Because...I'll have to consult my schedule,' Kira replied with dignity. She decided that Stefano was clearly far too used to getting everything his own way. Still, a chance to design the roof garden for a no doubt exceptionally beautiful town house in Florence...

'With the loss of the Bella Terra's owner, you're one client down. You've already said as much. I can fill that gap for you,' Stefano announced affably. 'You've already told me you hate canvassing for jobs and courting publicity. I've seen what you can do, and I'm offering you a valuable, long-term contract working for me. Where's the problem?'

The problem, Kira thought desperately, is you.

'I'm not sure I want to work for you, Signor Albani,' she said a little stiffly. 'We're so different. We might not get on.'

He trapped her gaze for a long time. 'What you mean is, you're afraid we might get on too well. And remember—my name is Stefano...' he added with a tempting smile.

Kira stared at him. His self-confidence was astonishing, and yet somehow she could not bring herself to resent it. He could read her mind—how could she criticise him for that?

'I appreciate your concerns, but you don't have to worry,' he went on. 'I have so many properties and projects, my contractors are dealt with mainly by email and text. I wouldn't be there in person to tempt you.' With that, his smile came dangerously close to laughter.

Kira had to look away. His body wasn't the only thing tempting her. She tried not to think of the begging letter, waiting for her on the table at home. There were so many calls on her slender finances. She needed money. The fabric of her house was so old there was always something that required repair. The security of a long-term contract appealed to her cautious nature. Her problem was, whenever she earned more than she actually needed she always felt bound to send any extra money back to England.

Her natural generosity might feel right, but she knew in her heart it was wrong. She would soon live to regret it, as she had done every single time in the past. What she earned ought to be hers to keep. She tried to harden her heart. It was difficult, and that was why she was such an easy target. Emotional blackmail was an ugly thing. Kira knew a steady contract to work for a billionaire like Stefano Albani would be a perfect new start. With that security behind her, maybe she could manage to make a stand. It would give her some badly needed confidence, and she could make sure that anything she did for Stefano would be strictly on her own terms. Yes, of that she was certain.

Well…almost certain…

'Your projects sound pretty interesting,' she told him carefully. 'When I get back home I'll check my diary, and see if I can fit you in somewhere.'

He gave her a calculating look. Then he dug a hand into his pocket and drew something out. 'Of course, I appreciate you can't give me an answer straight away. Here—take my card. I'll have my office draw up all the documents, and you can give them a call when you've come to a decision.'

His wallet was immaculate dark brown leather. The blue silk lining was no match for the intensity of his eyes as he pulled out a business card and handed it to her. Trying not to stare at it like a souvenir, Kira slid it into the pocket of her jeans.

'Thank you. I'll give it some serious thought.'

Lightning crackled. Kira braced herself, but the explosion of thunder still made her jump.

'It's getting closer.' She looked up at the sky, and then across at the horizon. It was as dark as an overripe plum. 'Are you sure you want to risk a tour of the estate in this weather, Stefano?'

'It will be fine.' He smiled. 'Trust me.'

That was the last thing Kira ever did. People always used that phrase as casually as they said 'to be honest.'

From that moment, she knew in her heart things would go wrong. She tensed, retreating into the role of observer as Stefano roamed around the formal gardens. Not content with admiring her work from the upper storeys of the house, he wanted information from ground level, too. He asked intelligent questions and paid her compliments about her work, but Kira could only let herself believe a fraction of his kind words. She moved uneasily under the shadow of his praise and flinched as the thunder grew closer. Finally, when they were at the furthest point of the tour, the rain began. Warm drops the size of pound coins darkened the dust, first in ones and twos, then in a downpour of tropical proportions.

'We'll head for there!' Stefano shouted over the torrents of rain. He was pointing at her cottage. 'It's the only blot on my landscape. We might as well make use of it before my men clear it away.'

'What?' Kira shrieked, but her horror was drowned by thunder roaring right overhead. They dashed for the house, but as they got closer Stefano faltered at the sight of garden flowers spilling through the woven hazel fencing.

'So someone lives here?' he shouted over the downpour.

'Yes—me!' Kira raced past him and flung open the door of her little retreat.

Breathless and soaked, they tumbled into the house.

'I didn't realise this estate came with a tenant,'

Stefano said as Kira kicked off her sandals and padded, dripping and barefoot, into the kitchen.

'It doesn't. I own La Ritirata outright,' Kira told him proudly as she returned, carrying a couple of hand towels.

'I wasn't aware of that. How much do you want for it?' Stefano looked at her quizzically.

'Oh, it's not for sale!' Kira laughed, running lightly up the wide stone stairs to fetch some larger towels from the airing cupboard. Stefano followed her for a few steps. Leaning back against the cream-painted stone wall, he looked up at her as she stood on the landing.

'Of course it is. Everything is for sale at the right price. You could find yourself a nice little hideaway in this valley, well away from La Bella Terra. Then we could each pretend we were totally alone in the landscape.'

'That's the point. There are no other houses—not for miles. That's partly why I love it here so much.'

'You could build yourself another paradise anywhere, Kira!' he went on. 'I've seen the proof, remember. Go on—name a figure. Anything you want, and it's yours.'

'All right, then—a million pounds!' Kira called down with a giggle.

'Done. I'll have my staff draw up the paperwork as soon as I get back to the office.'

Kira waited for him to laugh, but he didn't. He was in deadly earnest.

'You're joking!' she gasped. 'This place isn't worth a fraction of that sort of money!'

'My peace of mind is beyond price,' he announced.

Taken aback by the determination in his voice, Kira shook her head.

'Well, you may not have been joking, but I was. My house means the world to me,' she told him firmly. 'No amount of money would tempt me to give it up. La Ritirata gives me what I've always wanted—independence and contentment. I've worked hard for my little home, and I feel safe here.'

A tremendous blast of thunder rattled the windows. Stefano smiled.

'I notice you aren't so nervous, now we are within your own four walls,' he observed. 'You've obviously made a real commitment to this place.'

'I have.' She nodded, glad he appeared to have accepted she wouldn't be moving.

'In that case, I can't wait to benefit from the Bella Terra effect. I own a lot of investment properties around the globe, but I can't honestly call any of them home. If I see a place with potential, I buy it,' he told her, looking around her neat and compact little home appreciatively. 'Yet none of my houses have ever developed the comfortable, lived-in feeling of this place.'

'I spend as much time as I can here. Maybe that's the secret of my success.'

'It really works,' he said as she started back down the stairs towards him, holding out a huge fluffy towel. 'Living alone in a place like this, you must be as brave and resourceful as you are talented and beautiful.'

He reached out to her. As he took the towel from her hands, their fingers brushed against each other. His touch was light as an angel's kiss, but it sent lightning coursing straight through Kira's body. She gasped.

A thunderbolt crashed directly overhead, but neither noticed.

Stefano was looking deep into her eyes, and nothing else mattered.

CHAPTER FOUR

THE universe held its breath. Kira gazed at the gorgeous man standing just out of her reach. Her body ached to touch him. She could think of a million and one reasons why she should take that single step down into his arms. Only one thing stopped her. There was already a monumental mistake in her past. Kira was no longer the innocent girl she had once been, long ago and far away. She had forged a new life since then and almost learned to trust her instincts again, but she had never been faced by a choice like this before. Every fibre screamed at her to fall into Stefano's arms. At the same time, every cruel word and accusation she had suffered in the past kept her nailed to the spot.

Stefano came up a step to join her. Taking the towel from her hands, he draped it over her head. Very gently, he began massaging her hair dry. His light, sure touches made Kira wonder how many other women he had treated in this way. It was impossible to know. That was the danger. She knew what powerful men were like. They acted with confidence, and never left any room for refusal. She had the horrible fear that once she was in his arms he would give her no time to think. It would be bed, and then treachery. It might take a day, a week or a month before he deceived her, but the result would be the same. He would carry on as though nothing had happened. She would be totally crushed. It had happened to her once before, and Kira was not about to let herself become a victim again.

She put up her hands, shrinking back and trying to intercept his movements. His fingers closed over hers and gently pushed the towel back over her head. The clip securing her tumble of auburn hair fell away. It clattered down the staircase. Kira barely noticed. She was completely absorbed by the look in Stefano's eyes as he drew the towel away from her hair. The appreciation she saw was all for her. She began to tremble, but now it was with anticipation, not fear. She had never known such a wild yearning before.

She swallowed hard. There was nothing in her mouth but the taste of temptation. His eyes levelled a steady, questioning gaze, willing Kira to read what she wanted in them. It was mesmerising, but she could not escape the feeling of being confined in her own home. To take a step forward would lead straight into his arms. Kira refused to repeat her mistakes, and the irresistible Stefano Albani showed all the signs of being a disaster waiting to happen—to her.

She couldn't allow herself to fall under his spell.

'This is dangerous,' she said, forcing a laugh when he showed no sign of moving. 'Didn't you ever get told not to fool about on stairs?'

'No. But then, if I had I wouldn't be where I am today.'

Turning, he headed back down the stairs.

Kira was torn between relief and disappointment. When he walked away it was because he was unwilling to open up about himself. They had that in common, she recognised. It gave her enough courage to follow him downstairs. Although unable to take that one momentous step into his arms, she did not want to lose touch with him altogether.

'It's still pouring out there, Stefano. Why don't you stay for a coffee?' she ventured.

He did not look at her. Instead, he went over to the open front door. There he stood with one hand on either side of the door frame. When he spoke, his voice was as light and careless as hers.

'That would be great. And I meant what I said about wanting you to work for me.'

They might as well have still been discussing the weather. His attention was riveted on the curtains of rain rippling over her drenched and glittering garden.

'And I'm equally determined to take my time over considering your offer,' Kira said firmly, fixing him the macchiato he requested. She poured herself an identical drink, keen to keep a clear head while he was under her roof. 'I need to know what strings are attached, Stefano.'

'There won't be any. I like to keep my affairs simple.'

He was still watching the rain. As Kira reached his side with the coffee, the downpour wavered and began to ease. A final flurry of thunder rattled away into the distance.

'I like to keep my affairs completely separate from my work,' she said, handing him his cup.

He was silhouetted against the doorway, surveying the land beyond her garden fence as though it was already part of his very own kingdom. At last he turned his head and looked at her. A man who took control so naturally would never expect a woman to refuse him anything. That thought made Kira fizz with an illicit thrill. Stefano Albani might be about to buy the Bella Terra estate, but the power he had over her had nothing to do with territory. She felt the need for him growing within her. That desire was reflected in his beautiful blue eyes. His gaze was as tempting as evening sunshine. Kira knew she held the key to her own escape from solitude, and that made her powerful. She could choose to satisfy the cravings he was awakening in her body, or tighten her armour of self-reliance. The choice was hers and she was glad, but it disturbed her. It would be so easy to give in, right here and now. She was afraid that if she did, Stefano would turn out to be no better than the last man she had learned to trust.

Some dreams needed to be kept at arm's length. That way they could last for as long as she wanted.

As she passed Stefano the coffee, his fingers made contact with hers again. It was only for a fraction of a second, but it would linger in her memory for the rest of her life. Their eyes met as he drained the small cup in one movement. Then he walked over and placed it on the coffee table.

'The rain has stopped, so I must go. Thank you for being such a delightful hostess, Kira. I don't like to mix women and work, but as you aren't quite on my payroll yet...'

Before Kira knew what was happening she was in his arms. He took complete control as his body spoke for them both. His lips were cool and totally irresistible. She dissolved under the pressure, and he was there to catch her. Despite all her good intentions, she let herself reach out to him. She delighted in the delicacy of the thin, smooth skin stretched taut over his finely drawn cheekbones. Her fingers ran through the silkiness of his dark hair as she drew him ever closer to her, hungry to experience every nuance of him. In response, his fingers stroked lightly over her bare arms, forming a prison she never wanted to escape. When he began to draw away, she instinctively tried to follow. Gently, he detached her arms from his neck. Holding her hands between his, he squeezed them lightly.

'No. After what you have said to me today, Kira, I know you would never forgive yourself for mixing business with pleasure,' he said, his expression carefully innocent, but a wicked sparkle in his eyes belying his words. 'I'll tell my staff to get a draft contract out to you as soon as possible. Until then, goodbye.'

Lifting his hand to his lips, he blew her one final kiss, and then strode right out of her house.

It was all Kira could do not to rush after him. Fighting every instinct, she forced herself to stay exactly where she was. She wanted go out and wave him off, but a man like Stefano would see that as his right. Women were probably doing it every day of the week. It would do him good to think there was one woman who didn't keep him at the centre of her universe. The thought gave Kira a funny twist of pleasure, and she almost smiled. The racket his helicopter made as it roared into life was almost as hard to ignore as its pilot.

Kira only went out onto the veranda when the throbbing engine sound had dwindled away. Stefano's helicopter was high in the sky, reduced to the size of a child's toy. It made several slow circuits overhead like a bird of prey, and then headed off swiftly in the direction of Florence. This time she really did allow herself to smile.

Kira had run from romance for years. After that first disastrous affair with Hugh, she vowed never to get entangled again. And now Stefano Albani breezed into her life, attacking the walls of her reserve. She told herself it didn't matter, as the way she was feeling had nothing to do with love. Her heart was not involved. That meant there was no danger she could be hurt a second time. Her response to Stefano was on a purely physical level, and that was how she intended to keep it. He aroused her body to a pitch she had never before experienced. It was unprecedented, startling, but at least it was simple.

It was love that would complicate matters, and Kira had absolutely no intention of allowing that.

Stefano was a happy man as he flew back towards Florence. He hummed a snatch of Don Giovanni to himself, revelling in the comfort of his air-conditioned cockpit. The Bella Terra estate was what life was all about. That was why he worked so hard, and put up with all the long hours and pressure. His features sharpened with their usual hawklike intensity. Memory was a savage goad. Whatever he had to put up with, he could do it in luxurious surroundings waited on by dozens of staff. As a teenager he had heard English tourists talk of their villas in Tuscany and vowed he would live like them one day. Whatever they could do, he would do better. It had taken him nearly twenty years, but he had managed it. He was going to own the most beautiful valley in all Italy.

His blue eyes veiled. It contained the most beautiful woman in the country as well. The enigmatic Miss

Banks might well prove a bigger challenge than he had at first anticipated. Her failure to be swayed by his wealth or reputation made her unique, in his experience. A slow smile spread over his face the more he thought about her. Novelty wasn't the only reason why she leapt into his mind. Kissing her senseless had kindled a need for her within his body. The temptation to carry on softening her resistance beneath his lips and hands had been difficult to resist. It had threatened to overcome him, but he had conquered it. There was no shortage of sex in Stefano's life, but his reactions to Kira Banks felt somehow different. For once in his adult life, he was wondering less about her beautiful body, and more about the woman within.

He found himself wanting to see her again. That thought made him feel uneasy.

Miles away and far below, Kira shared his feelings. It had taken her so long to get over the horror that had been Hugh Taylor, she was determined never to be taken in by a man again. Yet Stefano Albani made her feel weak at the knees. And weak in the head, she told herself crossly, but it was impossible to think about him and frown. That was a revelation. Her only experience of men so far had ended in tears. Now, for the first time in years, a man was forcing her to reconsider. Stefano hadn't made her cry. In fact, every time she thought about him, she smiled. That will have to stop, she told herself sternly.

Memories usually knocked all the daydreams out of her head. Thoughts about Stefano didn't. Instead, she was filled with a wonderful warm feeling. It was such an unfamiliar sensation it took her a while to recognise

it as lust. Shy amusement engulfed her in a wave of embarrassment, but that vanished when she caught sight of
the envelope lying on her table. Stefano had stroked all
thoughts of it from her mind. She picked it up. Meeting
him put this letter from her stepparents into perspective.
If she could cope so well with a man like that, what
was to stop her dealing with a call from home? Full of
unusual optimism, she tore the envelope open. It was the
usual tissue-lined affair, drenched in her stepmother's
trademark perfume. Unfolding the stiff sheet of hand-
made paper, Kira cut straight to the chase. Glancing at
the foot of the letter, she read the words, 'All our love,
Henrietta and Charles.'

She scowled. That was all she needed to know. Her
stepparents only sent her their love when they wanted
money. If things were going well, they conveniently
forgot about the girl who had disappointed them in every
way, except in her capacity as a cash cow.

She scanned the rest of the copperplate handwriting.
Mr and Mrs Banks weren't stupid. They never came
straight out with a request for cash. Hints were threaded
through the glowing reports of their younger daughter
Miranda's success as an actress, and her new romance
with a millionaire. Of course, this meant the Banks
family wanted to entertain on a grand scale. Kira chuckled, imagining her stepmother circling Miranda's boy-
friend with canapés brought all the way from Fortnum
and Mason. They were her preferred bait for a future
son-in-law. The Bankses' mortgage was unpaid and their
house was falling apart. Despite that, the expensive perfume was still on draft and hopes of coming into money
from somewhere or another were still high. Some things
never changed.

Kira's face fell again as she read the final paragraph of the letter: 'When you ring each week, could you make it a little earlier? Six o'clock is such an inconvenient time as we're nearly always on the way out.'

Their instructions usually made her feel nine years old again, but today was different. Stefano Albani was stronger than all Kira's bad memories put together. Impulsively, she screwed up the letter and lobbed it towards the waste bin. It missed, but Kira was in good spirits as she got up to retrieve it. It was amazing what a little boost to the self-esteem could do.

And a kiss from Stefano Albani worked like rocket fuel.

Next day, Stefano's legal team presented him with a contract for the landscaping and design work he wanted done on his town house in Florence. His PA scheduled a call for him, summoning Miss Kira Banks to his office. While Stefano held meetings, Kira was pushed to the back of his mind. However, the moment he pulled her file from his in-box to make the call, things changed. At the sight of her name, he paused. One look at the neatly printed contract catapulted her to the front of his consciousness again. This wasn't some run-of-the-mill conquest. This was Miss Kira Banks, who had been funny and spiky and brought back powerful memories of the last time someone stood up to him. He found himself going back over every second of the previous day.

He inhaled deeply, bringing to mind the sweet lavender and lemon fragrance of her. She was perfumed by soap and fresh air. He spent a few moments revelling in her image. It was a mystery why she hid behind such a prickly attitude. He knew it was only a front. The warm surrender of her body beneath his hands when he touched her assured him of that. Her reactions were perfect. It was her mind he needed to explore. That idea made him uncomfortable.

Suddenly he leaned forward and snapped a button on his office intercom.

'Cancel that call, and the contract in the name of Kira Banks,' he growled. 'I need to do some more research.'

Stefano believed in being the best, and having the best. To keep up his high standards, he used only the top people. He wanted to employ Kira Banks because she really was the best person for the job, not just because he wanted to bed her.

Slumping back in his seat he gnawed the side of his thumb, deep in thought. Work and women were totally separate compartments of his life. He had fancied Kira from the first moment he saw her, but that was the very worst reason for giving anyone a job. Her work was great, but he had only seen one of her projects. For her body and spirit to haunt him like this, it could only be a bad thing. Emotion mustn't be allowed to affect his judgement. He ought to distance himself from the process, and get some other opinions. He needed to be absolutely sure she was the right person for this project.

Picking up his pen, he drew two careful lines through the name and address on the cover of the file in front of him. He liked speed, but not at the expense of perfection. Besides, that faint air of mystery surrounding Miss Kira Banks might erupt into some sort of scandal for Albani International. It didn't matter how Stefano wanted her, nothing could be allowed to taint the name of his company.

Not even the most beautiful Englishwoman in Italy.

Kira looked at Stefano's stark-white business card every day. Her heart fluttered with excitement. She ran her finger over the engraved wording until his telephone number was burned into her brain, but she never rang it. That smooth, self-assured man must never be in any doubt that Kira was her own woman, with other projects and a lot of things on her mind.

Finally, exactly two weeks after Stefano had grabbed her by mistake in the garden, she couldn't resist any longer. She sat down, cleared her throat and picked up the receiver. Then she put it down again. Maybe she should get her laptop up and running in case he started talking business straight away. She wanted him to think she was calm and efficient, even though she didn't feel it as she lifted the phone to try once more. This time she paused to fetch a glass of water. It would be terrible if her mouth dried before she could speak to him.

Eventually, her heart rattling like a touch typist's fingertips, she dialled the number.

'Signor Albani's office. How may I help you?' a sunny female voice enquired.

Kira had no idea. Naively, she'd thought the number on Stefano's own business card would have been a direct line to his desk.

'Who is speaking, please?' the voice asked as though she was only one among thousands.

'Kira Banks.' Kira made herself answer in the friendly, confident tone she reserved for clients. 'I'm ringing to check on a contract that Signor Albani was going to arrange for me.'

'Ah.'

That single sound was enough to bring her back to earth. While the receptionist went off to check, Kira was left to imagine exactly how many other women rang this number each day. Silver-tongued Stefano must make a million similar promises.

She was on hold for ages. The silence was almost as painful as piped music would have been. It gave her a long time to reflect on her foolishness. Finally, the receptionist returned, and Kira's heart fell still further.

'I'm sorry, Miss Banks, we have no record of a contract being issued in that name. Perhaps if you could give me a reference from the letter we sent you?'

'No…no. It's okay. I must have made a mistake,' Kira muttered indistinctly. And not for the first time, she thought bitterly as she put down the receiver.

Kira stared at the telephone for a long, long time. She felt totally deflated. In her daydreams, Stefano Albani couldn't wait to get back to her side. He would have paid cash for the Bella Terra estate, simply so he could move in as soon as possible. Instead, he must have forgotten about her the moment he climbed back into his helicopter. He had turned out to be no different from any of the other rich men she had worked for. All of them could spin a fine yarn. They couldn't make and hang onto big money without being able to charm investors. And women, she thought ruefully, touching her lips. Remembering the rasp of Stefano's cheek against her skin sent a tingle coursing through her body. She smiled, recalling the wonderful experience of being held and kissed until her worries spun away. The man was a rat, but why had she expected anything else?

She would cope. She had survived a worse disaster—and at least her brush with Stefano had happened in private. Her life was her own, and from now on that was how it would stay. She smiled sadly. Her single, unforgettable contact with him was a total one-off. It was destined never to happen again. I should have known that from the start, she told herself briskly.

She tried to smile again, but it was impossible.

Kira's disappointment over the contract squashed all her fantasies flat. No one did anything for nothing. Mentally she shrugged her shoulders, but Stefano refused to be forgotten. He had set such an exciting fire into her soul. Long ago, life had taught her to expect nothing when it came to men. She knew in her bones Stefano could be no different, but it had been a lovely fantasy. Those sweet memories of him refused to leave her. Whether drifting through her dreams or sending shock waves through her day when she thought she glimpsed his familiar figure in the street, Stefano would not let her go.

She was putting the finishing touches to a very chic project on the outskirts of Florence when her mobile rang.

'Miss Kira Banks?'

Kira couldn't recognise either the woman's voice, or the number that flashed up on her phone's screen. The only people who used this number were clients. Instantly on her guard, she hesitated.

'Who wants to know?'

'I work for Signor Albani. We understand you are on the point of completing a project for Prince Alfonse.

Signor Albani wants you to leave it and travel straight to his office. A car will pick you up in approximately—'

'Wait a minute!' Kira interrupted angrily. 'When I rang your office to check about this, you didn't even have any knowledge of a contract in my name!'

'When was this?'

'The day before yesterday.'

'Then perhaps you were a little impatient, Miss Banks.' The voice was cool.

Kira was in no mood to be treated like an idiot.

'If Signor Albani is clever enough to have found out where I'm working, then he ought to know better than to interrupt me when I'm busy. I don't have time to waste on idle chit-chat with an unreliable man.'

She heard a little gasp at the other end of the line. The voice became a shocked whisper.

'Miss Banks, what are you saying? No one refuses Signor Albani!'

'Well, I'm very sorry, but no one disappoints the person I'm currently working for, either. Especially not me,' Kira said firmly. 'And if you aren't willing to tell him that, maybe you could put me through to Signor Albani, direct?'

The woman wasn't happy, but put her on hold to see if the boss was taking calls. It gave Kira plenty of time to decide she had gone too far. She was being too emotional about this. Much as she hated to back down in any situation, where work was concerned she was a realist. She needed contracts. This one had the delightfully infuriating Stefano Albani at the other end, and that might make it more of a liability than a blessing. Autocratic behaviour was part of every billionaire's job description, but this particular man had got right under her skin. She wanted to be known for the quality of her work, not for making a fool of herself over a man.

Suddenly a voice purred in her ear.

'Kira, it's Stefano.' The sound was so deliciously accented, those few words were enough to wipe all the arguments from her mind.

'Hello,' she said, unable to think of anything else.

'You wanted to speak to me, Kira?'

'Yes.' Everything sensible and businesslike seemed to have been swept out of her head. She gave herself a mental shake. 'Thank you for having your secretary ring me, but I'm working on a very important project,' she snapped, hoping her brisk tone would put some distance between them again. 'I can't simply drop everything and rush to your side.'

'I know. You're a woman of spirit.' The laughter in his voice was infuriatingly engaging. 'Alphonse tells me you're practically finished at his place,' Stefano continued. 'I'm going to be out of the country for a while, and I wanted to discuss your contract with you, face to face, before I leave. I thought this would be a good opportunity for both of us,' he added.

Kira needed this job. She was also desperate to see Stefano again. After all, it does make good business sense, she told herself. There couldn't be any harm in a formal discussion. It would be like gazing at temptation through the window of a locked cake shop. Work would form an invisible shield between them, keeping her from disaster.

'You could be right...' She tried to sound grudging. 'How do I find you?'

She could hear his lack of surprise at her decision. 'Don't worry. I found you, don't forget. A car will be arriving to collect you…' There was a brief pause. Kira visualised him glancing at the designer watch clamped to his beautiful bronzed wrist as he added, 'In exactly fifteen minutes.'

And it was.

As her chauffeur-driven limousine glided to a halt at the main entrance of Albani International, Kira looked up at the grand old building with a hint of anxiety. It was enormous, and a constant stream of people flowed in and out of the revolving glass doors. A commissionaire stepped forward to open the car door for her. Thanking him, Kira took a few moments to compose herself before walking into the reception area. She had worked in palaces, villas and condos, but this place had something extra—Stefano Albani. Taking a deep breath, she went in to meet him.

To Kira's relief, there was no hanging around. That would have shredded her nerves beyond repair. She had been desperate to see Stefano again from the moment he left her house. Now she realised dreams were one thing, but reality was terrifying. The moment he spoke, her insides would turn to jelly. Her instinctive reaction was to keep her head down and pretend she was invisible, but that wasn't the way contracts were won. Instead, she lifted her chin, ready to meet his gaze with an equally bold stare. It took a huge effort.

The man of her dreams was lounging back in a big black chair. His feet were on his desk. He was dictating into a voice recorder and although his eyes instantly locked onto hers he did not stop speaking into it as she walked towards his visitor's chair.

Stefano looked every bit as intimidating as she

remembered. Despite his casual attitude, he was dressed in a beautifully cut dark suit. The formality of classically designed business wear suited him so well it was hard not to stare. Kira gave in to the temptation.

Completing his letter, Stefano switched off the recorder and tossed it aside.

'We meet again, Miss Banks.'

'Indeed we do.' Kira purposely kept her voice light and professional, but couldn't resist a question that had been tormenting her since he left her side. 'Did you buy the Bella Terra estate, *signore*?'

'Yes, but I've been too busy to visit since then. I suppose you've been wondering where I've been?'

'No, not at all,' Kira said coolly, determined not to betray any trace of the embarrassingly large amount of time she had spent wondering what he was getting up to while he was out of her sight.

She saw from a subtle change in his expression that the stony nature of her reply had given him pause. His reaction gave her a little lift, and added some real amusement to her smile.

'In fact, Signor Albani, when your assistant rang it took me a little while to remember who you were.' She batted the words easily across the desk at him.

He parried with a wicked smile. 'I knew you were one in a million, Kira. Now it seems you are unique.'

He took his feet off the desk and sat up straight in his chair, his suddenly businesslike attitude making him even more imposing. Kira fought to keep her expression impassive.

Don't overdo the flip answers! she thought. I might not want him to think he means anything to me, but he is a man who managed to borrow me from Prince Alfonse!

'I want you to work for me, Kira. Name your price,' he drawled, glancing down as he threaded a pair of solid-gold cufflinks into his cuffs.

'I'd rather find out what I'm letting myself in for first.' Kira was proud of the careful neutrality of her tone. It was a shame the rest of her being was entirely focused on the man she had been fantasising about for the past few days. 'I want to make sure I'm the right person for the job. I'd rather you offered the position to someone else if I thought I couldn't give you exactly what you wanted.'

'I agree completely,' Stefano said. 'However, I wouldn't have asked you here today were I not already certain. You, Kira Banks, are capable of giving me *exactly* what I want.' His face remained expressionless but the ambiguity of his words made her cheeks flush red and her breathing catch.

In a quick, carefully judged gesture he spun the file across the desk at her. 'So why don't you read that, and tell me what you think?'

Kira did not move, but regarded him coolly.

'What? Now?'

Stefano raised an eyebrow. 'Unless you have some objection?'

Kira had spent too many restless hours since their first meeting. After her roller-coaster ride of hope, disappointment and surprise, she did not find his words at all funny.

'No. This is so important to me, and it deserves to be studied carefully. I take my work very seriously,' she said slowly, trying to gauge his reaction.

Stefano nodded appreciatively. 'That's exactly the sort of attitude I expect from the people I employ. It's why I want you on board. I had my staff check out some of the other projects you've completed. I needed to make sure I was offering you work for all the right reasons, not simply the wrong one.'

His smile became enigmatic and Kira had to look away. She transferred her gaze back to the cover of the file in front of her. If he paid such careful attention to detail, she wondered what else his people might have found out about her.

'Could you give me an overview?' she said eventually. 'Isn't it simply a contract to work on the gardens at Bella Terra?'

'That, and my Florentine town house as well...'

It had been at the back of Kira's mind, but she'd hardly dared hope he would remember his casual offer.

'Words are cheap. Nobody knows that better than I do, Stefano. Men often say things they don't mean,' she said quietly.

He stared at her. 'Not when it comes to business. Honesty is the only policy there,' he said firmly. 'Since we met and I've had such favourable reviews of your work, I thought I'd raise the stakes. This contract offers you employment not only at Bella Terra, and Florence, but also on my new property in the Caribbean.'

Kira could have bounced straight up to the ceiling in sheer delight. It sounded like her dream contract. Instead, she frowned and bit her lip. 'I've never worked in the Caribbean.'

'Then you're in for a treat. It will be a wonderful experience,' Stefano assured her. 'Silver Island has everything. One hundred hectares of tropical wilderness surrounded by beaches as fine as sugar, set in a warm blue sea.'

Despite her determination to play it cool, Kira's eyes sparkled.

'It sounds lovely already,' she said wistfully.

Stefano had no illusions. He frowned. 'I thought so, too, when I first bought it. But despite all the luxury there's still something lacking. It'll be your job to make the whole place more—' he grimaced, so used to total satisfaction that he couldn't find the words to identify the problem '—user-friendly,' he said eventually, but looked no happier with the phrase than Kira felt.

'That doesn't give me much of a clue.' She shrugged.

'Silver Island is a perfect hideaway. No expense was spared in setting it up, and yet—' he ran his fingertip pensively across his lips '—for all its qualities, it lacks something. I want to import the magic you have worked on the Bella Terra estate. In the same way that you can live in the town house here in Florence while you're working on it, you could stay in the Caribbean while you restructure Silver Island. You'll be on the spot, all the time.'

And where will you be? Kira was appalled to find herself thinking.

'I don't suppose you noticed exactly how interested I was in your garden?' Stefano continued.

'I did,' Kira said, trying to concentrate on their moments of light, insubstantial chit-chat and forget the instant he took her in his arms. It was hopeless. The way she felt about him surged into her mind again. The force of his presence overwhelmed every other memory. A tiny tremble in her voice betrayed her. He noticed, and suddenly his devastating mouth curled up at the corners.

'Yes, I can see....'

All Kira's worries about the Bella Terra valley faded. The intensity of his stare focused on her to the exclusion of everything else. He looked like a tiger ready to pounce. The tremble extended throughout her body and she felt her self-control slipping away into warm arousal. It gathered in all her most feminine places, waiting for one word, one movement from him, to unleash its power.

'Good...so as soon as you're happy with your contract, we'll be on our way.'

'Where?' Kira asked faintly.

Stefano put his elbows on the desk and netted his fingers. 'To Silver Island—you'll need to experience the place in all its glory before you can hope to do it justice. The computer hasn't been built that can give you the experience of warm sand between your toes, and swaying palms beneath a tropical sky.'

The words flowed from him like the tropical breezes he spoke of—warm, gentle and so very seductive.

CHAPTER FIVE

KIRA wanted this job more than anything else in the world, but if she was honest with herself, working so closely with Stefano would be dangerous. How was she supposed to keep her mind on her job? Travelling around the world with him would be torture. It wouldn't simply be a case of storming off down the road if she felt herself weakening. She would be a long way from home and completely at the mercy of a man who held her spellbound. It was the same old story from her university days. Kira couldn't face falling into that trap again. A man like Stefano could never commit to just one woman—that much was obvious from his easy smile and delicious kiss. No woman with any sense should trust him with her heart.

Kira didn't know what to do. Surely if she was aware of the danger, that would make it easier to avoid? And a business contract was legally binding. It meant security. She rated that highly. The problem was, working for Stefano was bound to be a temptation too far. She had no confidence in her ability to resist him, and the man was trouble with a capital T. Her heart had spent the past few days on a helter-skelter of hope and gloom, and it was all his fault. Even if she kept her distance from him, working together would mean seeing exactly how faithless he could be from day to day. That would be a thousand times worse.

'I know—let's leave business behind and I'll take you to lunch first. We can discuss it further there, if you like?'

Kira put her hands on her chair and shifted her weight back a little in the seat. Her feelings were all over the place. She needed to draw some boundaries between the two of them, make it clear that she wouldn't simply fall into line. Everything was moving so fast. She blurted out, 'I won't be rushed. Please don't take me and my feelings for granted.'

He drew back across his desk, and stared at her. It wasn't often possible to read his expression, but Kira thought she saw a brief flash of astonishment.

'Is that what you think I'm doing? Is that how it feels to you?'

She braced herself for an explosion of rage, and answered him defiantly.

'Yes. Yes, it does.'

The expected outburst never came. Stefano simply looked at her thoughtfully. Kira gained a little confidence from that.

'What else would you call it?' she added, more boldly. 'Before you left my home, you promised me great things. It was a good job I didn't believe you, because all I got was radio silence. When I finally rang your office to check on whether there was a contract in the name of Kira Banks, there was no trace—'

Stefano couldn't resist interrupting. 'That was only because I wanted time to double-check your work, and to be completely sure you were the right person to—'

'Please! Let me finish.'

Surprised into silence, he met her scowl with raised eyebrows. Then, with a nod, he raised both his hands as a sign she would be allowed to carry on without any more interruptions.

'You seem to be expecting me to obey you without question, Stefano, and I won't have it,' she said bluntly.

His clear blue eyes watched her steadily, and then he suddenly nodded.

'I'll take that into consideration.' He frowned a little before continuing. 'That took courage. So that we both know where we stand, Kira, maybe I should tell you that no employee has ever got away with speaking to me like that before.'

She opened her mouth to say something, but the way he began to smile stopped her.

'My relationship with contractors, on the other hand, can be rather more—' he lowered his lids slightly, hooding those beautiful eyes '—easy-going, shall we say?'

She stared at him. When he looked at her like that, she couldn't have gone on scolding him if her life depended on it.

'You don't have to make any allowances for me,' she murmured, suddenly and mysteriously short of breath.

Stefano shook his head sagely. 'I admire you for making a fresh start in a new country. A heart in pain is too often the cause of endless trouble.'

He was probing. Kira could tell. When she thought of the research he had done on her, it made her edgy. Had he stuck to her work, or had he delved into more personal areas? The uncertainty made her nervous, so she refused to be drawn any further.

'I bet you've created a fair few broken hearts your-self!' she parried with a laugh. She thought he would do the same, but his reaction was quite different. Instead, he stood and roamed over to the window.

'You could say that. When I was younger, I saw too much abuse to put any faith in human relationships. Instead, I turned my back on all the fine old Italian bonds of family. Escape cost me so much, I'm never going there again.'

Standing at the window, hands on hips, he stared out over the busy cityscape like an eagle searching for prey. His words hinted at an inner pain of his own. Kira's heart went out to him, but it would take a lot of nerve to approach a man who so obviously shunned sympathy.

'I'm sorry,' Kira said softly, after a pause. 'It's terrible to grow up where you aren't wanted.'

Stefano's answer shrugged off her concern.

'That's why I made sure I didn't.' He spoke to the pane of glass in front of him. 'I kept right out of every-one's way. From that moment I started working, and never stopped. It was around the clock, and all year long. It saved me from having to go back home.'

Suddenly he clapped his hands with a loud report that made her jump. 'But what are you doing to me, Kira?' His easy smile returned as he swivelled around and strode back to his desk. 'I didn't bring you here to dissect my private life! I brought you here to talk busi-ness, and enjoy a working lunch. Then we'll go and see my town house.'

Kira's own experience of a loveless childhood made her wonder about his past. Then Stefano's eyes con-nected with hers and wiped the thought clean out of her head. She recognised a heart-stopping shadow of the longing she had seen when he left her. Confused, she picked up the file containing her contract. She wanted to sign, and yet such close contact with the gorgeous Stefano was bound to put her self-control under impossible strain. To her, surrender meant dangerous dependency. She had seen her stepmother and her stepsister fall prey to it. Once a man took over their lives, they stopped seeing themselves as individuals. Kira could not bear to lose a part of herself like that.

'Did you take Amanda the estate agent out to dinner when you signed the final paperwork on Bella Terra?' Her question was as mild as mustard.

There was silence. Made brave by it, she looked up at him sharply. Expecting to find him looking guilty, she was disappointed.

'Would it make any difference to you, Kira?'

His face was impassive. It was another probe. That only made her wonder all the more. He hadn't denied a liaison with the woman, although if he had, Kira would have assumed he was lying.

'Maybe,' she mused, trying to look and sound casual as she studied the closely typed document for snares and pitfalls. 'I don't like men who use their position in life as a lever for their sexual conquests. I like to keep my work and my private life strictly separate.'

'You told me as much the other day. I'll bear it in mind,' he said gravely, but then his mouth twitched. 'So in future, there will be absolutely no business talk whenever I visit your house after moving into La Bella Terra.'

The thought of inviting Stefano over the threshold of her home raised Kira's temperature in a frighteningly exciting way. She cleared her throat, trying not to squirm in anticipation. Her lips became dry, and she had to moisten them with her tongue before announcing, 'I think we ought to get one thing straight right from the start, Stefano. I'm a genuine loner. I don't fancy the idea of you dropping into my home at odd hours while I'm off duty, distracting me with…talk,' she finished awkwardly.

His reply was so simple, it shocked her. 'That's a shame.'

She looked up, waiting for him to try and persuade her otherwise. His face was as poker fit as her own as he added, 'Now come on, let's have lunch.'

Kira stood, mentally preparing herself. Lunch with Stefano was sure to be the stuff of fairy tales. That worried her. Powerful people liked to create a good impression—to begin with. They showered you with pixie dust until you were dazzled into falling in with their plans.

'I'd be delighted, but don't expect me to sign this contract on the strength of it. I'd rather my legal people had a good look at it before I make a final decision,' she said airily.

Kira's only advisers were her cynical nature and a glass of pinot grigio, so she was rather looking forward to that consultation.

'Good. That leaves us free to discuss much more interesting things over lunch.' He smiled, pulling on his jacket as he led her to the door. 'Although I'm rather surprised a forthright woman like you doesn't go through her own paperwork!'

She smiled as he strode across his office and opened the door to let her out.

* * *

Kira's journey to the ground floor couldn't have been more different from her trip up to the executive suite. Then, she had spent every second checking her appearance. Now she kept her eyes riveted on the thick cream carpet. It wasn't that she didn't know where to look. She desperately wanted to gaze at Stefano, but somehow she couldn't do it. She had to be content with hints of his aftershave or the jingle of change in his pockets as he stood so close to her, yet so distant.

A limousine was waiting for them outside the revolving doors of the office block. Its driver opened the door for Kira. She slid in, glad of the excuse not to have to look at Stefano as he exchanged a few words with his driver.

He was every bit as good as her fantasies. His first words to her when she walked into his office had been absolutely right. The past few days had tortured, tormented and distracted her with thoughts of what he had been doing, and with whom. Stefano was the only man who had ever moved her like this. It made her certain he must have a new girl every night. Who could possibly resist that clear-eyed gaze? Kira was terribly afraid she couldn't. Her pulse increased to dizzying levels each time he looked at her. As he took his seat beside her in the car it felt as though her heart was trying to jump into her throat. Her mouth went dry, and she felt heat pool in the pit of her stomach.

It had been hard enough not to reach out to him when he had been standing alone and aloof in his office stronghold. How much more difficult would it be to resist him when they were at lunch together?

'When it comes to that contract, you'll have no worries,' Stefano said as their car pulled out into the stream of traffic outside the headquarters of Albani International. 'I'm ruthless in business, but I'm always fair. That agreement is simple, straightforward and totally unthreatening. Working for me will be the smartest move you ever make. I've seen the design work and planting you did on the Bella Terra estate, and I've heard brilliant reports from your other clients. Your touch is exactly what I need. You'll bring your talents to my properties around the world. In return, I'll reward you well and give you free advertising among all my contacts. That will save you all the tiresome brown-nosing for business you hate so much. Think of it—all the work you could ever want, but none of the socialising.'

He slid a smile towards her. Kira thought of the man she had seen silhouetted against the cityscape. His expression tangled her heartstrings before her brain had time to intercept it.

'You don't know what that would mean to me,' she said, the relief of getting work without having to pitch for it filtering through her words. Whenever she was in Stefano's presence, her body refused to behave. It ignored all the warning signs. Her brain screamed *danger* but her soft, warm feminine core heard only *temptation* and remembered only their kiss.

'We're here,' he said, sounding slightly husky, and Kira wondered if he was struggling with similar memories, but he leapt out of the car before she could see his face. By the time he had arrived to open her door, he was back to business.

'This is one of my favourite restaurants,' he explained as he escorted her into a beautiful old building in the heart of the city. Its glamorous receptionist was all teeth and talons. She greeted Stefano by name, and led them to a spacious table for two. It was like no business lunch Kira had ever attended. As a respected professional she was used to being treated well. Stefano's idea of entertaining was in an entirely different league. The Michelin-starred restaurant was as perfect as its extensive menu, and Kira felt entirely uncomfortable. She looked down the list of tempting dishes, studying the menu intently, but it was no good. Eventually, she had to swallow her pride. It stuck in her throat, but as a regular Stefano was the best person to ask for help. 'I'm sorry. This is a cordon bleu restaurant and I'm a cucina povera girl at heart. All these exotic things are way out of my zone. Which do you recommend?'

'Definitely the lamb. It's a favourite of mine.'

Her mind made up, Kira ordered and handed her menu to the waiter.

Stefano ordered the same for himself, and a bottle of wine to accompany their meal. When they were alone again, he leaned towards her. His eyes were keen with interest.

'I would have thought a woman such as yourself would be entertained in restaurants like this all the time,' he said quietly. 'You deserve the best.'

Kira withdrew from the intensity of his gaze. 'I've told you—I enjoy plain Italian food.'

Stefano smiled suddenly. 'You are very much an Englishwoman. None of them are any good at truly indulging themselves.'

Clearly, thought Kira wryly, *he's never met my mother.*

'There aren't any fish-and-chip shops in the Bella Terra valley, so I've learned to adapt a little!' she said, relaxing in spite of herself as she looked around at their luxurious surroundings. 'It makes it easier when you bring me to a wonderful place like this. Everything is so beautiful, especially that dessert trolley over there. Mmm, I do so love my puddings!' She laughed, suddenly overcome with amazement at where she was and who she was with.

The waiter delivered their main course, and the glorious scent helped to relax her further. She ate a forkful and almost moaned in pleasure. Stefano watched her appreciatively. There was something suspiciously predatory in his eyes, but, overwhelmed and exhausted from fighting her attraction to him, when he held her gaze Kira didn't look away. He smiled slowly and she felt her hunger change into a more immediate desire.

'I wonder if this is a good time to tell you I haven't thought about another woman since we met,' he murmured slowly, in a voice silken with charm.

'It wasn't the thinking I was worried about!' Kira sighed reflexively before snapping her mouth shut and blushing bright red. Too late, she corrected herself. 'If I was worried at all, which I'm not.'

His voice became a caress. 'That's good. I wouldn't want to worry you, Kira. The fact is, you intrigue me. I've spent the time since I left your side wondering about you, pure and simple.'

'I'll bet there was nothing remotely pure or simple about it,' she retorted, although it was hard to stay angry with a man who gazed into her eyes with such intensity.

Her tone had definitely mellowed. Stefano picked up on it. He put down his fork. For a moment his hands spoke for him. The fingers spread wide, his wrists rolled from side to side on the edge of the table.

'Why block me when I'm trying to tell you something,

Kira?' His words were quiet, but intense. 'Let me into your life a little. You won't regret it. I can do things for you that you would never dream were possible. With your skill and my backing, there is no limit to what can be achieved. I want to start finding my pleasure much closer to home, and you are the one who can make it happen.'

Transfixed by his expression, Kira let him slide his hand over hers as it lay on the table. Incapable of re-sisting him, her fingers went limp. He began to stroke the back of her hand. His movements teased her with thoughts of how he had held her willing body against his only two weeks before. From the second he swept out of her front door, he left a yawning void in her life. She had spent so little time with him, and yet over those long, lonely days she had missed him so much. Kira felt every moment she didn't spend gazing into his eyes must be wasted.

A rising tide of emotion stirred her restlessly in her chair. Fine dining was nothing to the thought of Stefano making love to her. Suddenly she wanted him as ur-gently as she had desired him that day in her house. The colour of his eyes mirrored her needs. Beneath the long, flowing tablecloth she felt the slight movement of his foot as it slipped between hers. It happened as easily as his bare limbs might caress and possess her own.

'The moment you agree to work for me and sign that contract, I shall take you to Silver Island and show you my new paradise. Sun, sand and warm blue waters. It is everything you deserve, *cara mia*…' he whispered. His voice slipped over the words like a lazy tide lap-ping over land. Kira felt the last vestiges of her common sense slipping away. It was the powerful seduction in his eyes....

She passed the tip of her tongue over her parched lips.

'Stefano...I...'

The yapping of a pocket dog at the reception desk broke the spell. Kira blinked as though waking from a dream. As she came to her senses she saw an unmistakable look pass across Stefano's face. He might be a master at hiding his feelings, but he wasn't quite quick enough to conceal them from her. He was anticipating something. She looked across the busy restaurant. An impossibly tall, thin blonde was handing over her designer shoulder bag. The head of a noisy chihuahua poked out of it like a ripe russet apple. Relieved of the sum total of her responsibilities, the blonde turned around and surveyed the restaurant as though she was at the end of a catwalk. After jiggling a hand at several acquaintances, her eyes fastened on the table where Kira and Stefano were sitting.

In a cacophony of sleek designer fabric and six-inch heels she sashayed towards them. Kira tensed. Unconsciously her fingers went to her hair, then her smart but simple jacket, smoothing down its creases and fiddling with the buttons.

'Ah, Chantal!' Stefano turned as the woman got nearer.

Kira couldn't see his face, but heard his smile and could imagine the rest.

'Darling Stefano!'

With a winning smile especially for her, Stefano abandoned his plate and stood up. Greeting the blonde as though he was used to interruptions like this, he showed more style than Kira's one and only lover had ever done. She wondered how many times a seasoned philanderer had to run through this routine before it became second nature. Stefano had obviously put in the hours. He had turned it into an art form. Grasping his friend Chantal by the elbows, he air-kissed her with great pleasure.

'It's been a while, Stefano!' The blonde returned his gesture, running cool blue eyes over Kira's clothes and hair in a way that didn't simply give Kira a hint, it dug her savagely in the ribs.

Stefano was totally unfazed. Taking Chantal's hand, he pulled her fingers towards his lips for a real kiss. 'How was Biarritz?'

Chantal sighed theatrically. 'Nothing without you, darling, of course! Aren't you going to introduce me to your new friend? I haven't seen you about before, have I?' she said, giving Kira a bright, shiny look.

'Kira is a business associate,' Stefano said with barely a flicker.

'Pleased to meet you.' Chantal sent her a vague smile which failed to reach her eyes, before turning her attention back to Stefano.

Kira wasn't fooled for a moment. There was sympathy in that look. It told her—loud and clear—that Chantal didn't see her as any sort of threat. That made her feel more alone than she had ever done in her life. Chantal and Stefano, two of the beautiful people, chatted easily about friends she knew only as employers. Several times, Stefano tried to include Kira in their conversation, but she was simply too self-conscious and had nothing to say. She sat in mortified silence until Chantal left. When Stefano turned his full attention back to her again, she couldn't meet his eyes. She looked down hurriedly at her meal.

He introduced me as his 'business associate,' she thought, catching sight of herself in the glittering silver cutlery. *That really puts me in my place. I suppose I should be glad—it saves me having to worry about getting jumped on at every opportunity.*

At least it meant she could sign that contract safe in the knowledge nothing more than work would be on offer.

Somehow, having seen Stefano in action as he charmed Chantal, that didn't feel like such a good thing any more.

He went back to his meal as though nothing had happened. Kira was left to burn with embarrassment in silence. She tried to console herself that an affair with Stefano would be like this all the time. There would be constant interruptions from glamorous women in designer dresses. It would be Kira's idea of hell on earth.

After savouring another mouthful of lamb, Stefano looked up and smiled at her again.

'Now, where were we?' he said in a confiding murmur.

Kira put her heart and soul into a dazzling smile. It was the only way she could speak without screaming.

'I was about to tell you I wasn't in the ego-massaging business, Stefano. I've been fooled by a plausible rogue once before and I've got no intention of being caught out a second time, thank you!'

A look came into his eyes that she could not name, but it definitely wasn't remorse.

'I never for one moment imagined you would be,'

he said, looking so serious that she knew straight away he was telling the truth. 'Although you've touched on something I've been unable to get out of my mind since I met you at Bella Terra. When we were talking the other evening, it sounded as though you left England under a cloud. If you feel able, I would like to know more about what happened.'

Kira stared at him. His eyes hadn't left her since he said goodbye to Chantal. He had never once looked over his shoulder to see what the other woman was doing. *Whatever she might have been to him in the past, he's gazing at me now,* she thought in a desperate attempt to steady her nerves. She thought of everything that had happened over the past two weeks. Throwing away that begging letter from her stepparents had been a wonderfully freeing gesture. She remembered how close she had come to unburdening herself upon their first meeting. It was so tempting to let him in, to give Stefano a tiny insight into her problems. She took a deep breath, trying to summon up the courage to shed a little more light onto her murky past.

'Yes, I did—but the cloud wasn't of my making,' she began, but the memory of Chantal's contemptuous gaze and how separate a world Stefano came from shook her, and at the last moment she could not bring herself to go into details. 'Although I helped make it into the thunderstorm that sent me scuttling over here. I was escaping a disastrous affair. I abandoned the rat, and started all over again. I found myself a new life, and made a new start.'

Realising she would go no further, Stefano nodded. 'I might have guessed. There are two sorts of people—

those who crumble at the first hint of disaster, and those who conquer it and thrive.'

'I didn't exactly bounce back the next day,' Kira said ruefully, waving away his concern. 'But you're right—drawing a line under my mistake was the best thing I did. It let me move on. I took stock of my life, and then decided to apply for a course in horticulture. I've always liked working with plants, and it turned out I had quite a talent for it. One thing led to another so fast I was exhibiting before the world at Chelsea within three years. Shortly after that I found my home in La Ritirata. I've been here ever since.'

'And achieved wonders.' Stefano leaned forward and quietly pushed a strand of hair behind her ear. Kira melted. It would be so easy just to lean forward and kiss him…. In less than an hour he had delighted, infuriated and confused her, sometimes all at once. She could hardly think straight. Then, from the other side of the room, she heard Chantal's laugh and suddenly tensed.

Maybe she's laughing at me, she thought, hopelessly hypnotised by a consummate seducer. If they're not laughing now, then surely it's only a matter of time….

That was all it took. Her mind cleared, but her words were unsteady. 'I thought we came here to talk about work, Stefano?'

Lifting his glass of wine to her in a silent toast, he treated her to a devastating smile.

'Yes, but there's no need to restrict ourselves, Kira.'

Colour rushed into her cheeks. The days fell away and once again she was in his arms, her hands hungry for his perfectly formed body. The powerful bulk of him was so close she could have reached out and touched him.

Right now his body was hidden beneath the beautifully tailored lines of a white shirt and business suit, but the look in his eyes concealed nothing. He expected to take her to his bed. He demanded nothing less—and Kira wanted nothing more.

CHAPTER SIX

SHE fought to remain calm. Stefano wanted her, she wanted him—but she didn't need all the problems that would bring. He had affected her deeply from the moment they met. Bitter experience told her that was dangerous. She didn't want her illusions about him shattered by getting too close. He was bound to break her heart. She knew it. What happens when he dumps me—as he will, sooner or later? she asked herself. When he moved into La Bella Terra he would be living only a few hundred metres from her front door. Becoming the heartbroken doorstop of a faithless philanderer was definitely not on her 'to do' list.

Obviously deciding he'd let her suffer for long enough, Stefano seamlessly changed gear.

'How do you feel about house-hunting? With access to my contacts, the world really is your oyster. If you see anything that takes your fancy, let me know. There's no limit.'

Just as Kira felt herself taking off, Stefano's words brought her back to earth. Grateful for the chance to nail her feet back to the ground again, she interrupted him quickly.

'I hope you aren't trying to buy me out again. I'm

happy living right where I am, in the house I've made my own, in the perfect position.'

Stefano said nothing, but his slowly widening smile was enough to make her body move uneasily beneath its warmth.

'You are a stubborn woman. You have integrity and determination. Work with me and I can assure your future. It isn't only a matter of beautifying my own properties. My company, Albani International, has a charitable arm which is involved in all sorts of exciting projects. I was deeply impressed when I saw the work you have done at Bella Terra. Once you have finished working on my homes, you can start bringing your influence to bear in many other places.'

'I'm glad you've got such confidence in me.' Kira blushed, her clear skin for a moment matching the intricate strawberry meringue the waiter set before her.

Stefano's sensual lips parted in a half-smile as he saw Kira's delight in the summery confection of pinks and white on the dish laid in front of her.

'Look, why don't we visit my apartment after we finish here? You can see where you'll be working, if you decide to sign that contract. I told Prince Alfonse not to expect you back today.'

'Oh, you did, did you?' Kira said archly, inspired by a sugar rush. 'I hope you also told him we're out on business.'

Stefano didn't answer. His expression was telling Kira everything she didn't want to know, but her conscience was clear. For the moment, at least.

'As it happens, I think visiting the site is a very good idea,' she added coolly. 'I never accept a job until I have made a thorough study beforehand.'

'Good. I'm all for close scrutiny,' he said. With a nod of his head he summoned the head waiter, who brought a bottle of chilled champagne to their table. When it had been poured out, Stefano lifted his glass to her in another toast.

Kira remembered the last time he looked at her like that. It was in the split second before he kissed her. His eyes had a way of stripping away everything from her soul. She tried telling herself that he must size up every one of his female conquests like this, but a viper's nest of conflicting responses writhed within her body. His smile held out all sorts of possibilities. That was what made him so dangerous. At least she had no illusions, and could be on her guard.

'To our new partnership,' he said, his voice a sensual growl of anticipation which immediately created answering ripples in the pit of her stomach. Determined to quell them, she snapped

'Are you always so openly provocative?'

He broke the tension with a sudden laugh. 'I've never met another woman quite so woundingly honest! I can't help it, I'm afraid. Some men are born to it, while others need to be coaxed out of their shell by a loving, sensitive hand.'

Kira felt colour riot in her cheeks. Before she could explode, Stefano turned his statement into a warning.

'I am most definitely not one of those men.'

Stefano's town house was such a short distance from the restaurant he didn't bother calling up his driver. They walked. Kira had difficulty in keeping up with his long strides as he led her through the narrow streets. Without a word he fell back in step with her. Crossing a sunlit square, he directed her into a narrow canyon between two impossibly high and ancient stone walls. Kira looked around nervously as they left the sun-drenched crowds and plunged into shady solitude. Suddenly she realised he was no longer at her side. With a start, she swung around. He stood beside a pair of large wooden gates, let into the anonymous wall. With one hand he turned the wrought-iron handle in a small pass door and pushed it open.

'We're here. Go ahead.'

Kira cast one last apprehensive look up and down the narrow alley.

'Why are you so nervous? This is the best part of town.' He chuckled. 'Anyone would think I was trying to abduct you.'

A crazy vision of Stefano sweeping her away into the desert on a spirited Arab stallion flashed into Kira's mind. That threw her into confusion, but her mind cleared the instant she stepped into his courtyard. It was like standing at the bottom of a dry well. High walls irregularly perforated by small barred windows closed in on every side. This was a place the sun only reached when it was directly overhead. The building was ancient and beautiful, but putting a garden here would require imagination and skill. When he first mentioned a town house, Kira's mind had started playing with the idea of a private sun terrace. This place offered all the privacy anyone could want, but none of the rays.

'Good grief,' she whispered to herself, before adding aloud, 'This is going to be a challenge.'

He looked concerned. 'If you think it's going to be too much for you, tell me. I'll get someone to steam clean the whole place and leave it at that.'

'No!' Kira left his side and began pacing out the stark, stony area. 'There's nothing I enjoy more than a challenge. I'm not a quitter. If something can be imagined, it can be achieved.'

'Like a holiday home on Mars, maybe?'

Kira ignored him. Rummaging in her bag for a notebook and pencil, she began scribbling instead.

'I'll tell you what I like—' Stefano began, but she shook her head.

'This will only work if I tell you what is feasible first. Then you can choose which plants from my list you prefer.'

Stefano lodged his hands on his hips. 'What happened to "the client is always right"?'

Kira snapped her notebook shut, looked up and stared at him. He stared back. Despite her flinty expression, her mind was moving like quicksilver. This was one argument she could not afford to lose. Stefano could be infuriating, but he was offering her a series of lucrative contracts. He was also close to irresistible, and very easy on the eye. As long as she could harden her heart to stay out of his clutches, this would be a dream appointment. This site presented huge problems, but Kira would enjoy overcoming them. It gave her an unbeatable feeling to see a satisfied client, especially when it was a job other firms might consider too difficult. And she would be working for Stefano. The idea remained deliciously dangerous. She decided on a trial run.

'Fine. You're right—I'm not going to argue with you,' she announced. 'As long as you settle my bills, I'll do whatever you want. I can't guarantee you will be perfectly happy first time, though. The only plants that have a chance of surviving here are the sorts chosen specifically for these conditions. Unless you do as I say, you may end up with plants that have to be replaced every few weeks, because they die.'

'That's not a problem.' He shrugged.

'It is for me. I'm no tree hugger, but I can't stand the thought of all that waste. I'd rather we worked together as a team from the start and got this right straight away. Wouldn't you?'

'When you put it like that...' he reasoned.

Kira smiled. 'Great. My own website has a facility for choosing the right plant for the right place. I'll take you through the process, and then you'll be able to download the selection and spend as long as you like choosing what you want. The final decision will always be yours.'

His eyes narrowed. 'I know. That's why I'm looking forward to co-operating with you. Why don't we go inside? I can check out your suggestions, and try to soften a few of your rough edges at the same time.' He showed her towards the main door of his house.

Stefano ordered coffee and invited Kira into a stark, brightly lit office on the ground floor. It was full of the best and most expensive computing equipment, and the school-room stink of exam papers, solvents and printing ink. She recoiled. It was too sharp a reminder of the days when every exam success meant she was subject to more sneering at home.

With a computer logged in, Stefano stood to let her take his place at the keyboard. Kira called up her website. The moment he saw it, he looked impressed. That gave her confidence a big boost.

'I want to feel the same affection you have for your

own home,' he said, leaning over the back of her chair.
'I enjoy property, yet somehow it never turns out to be
the pleasure I expect it to be. Whenever I buy anything,
it is a rock-solid investment,' he said, but with an unusual
lack of enthusiasm.

Kira was so surprised by the note in his voice, she
swivelled her chair around to face him.

'You don't sound convinced, and I can't say I'm surprised. I don't care what my cottage on the Bella Terra
estate is worth, but I suppose it will be a lot less than I
paid for it.'

'You're right. For once, I don't seem to care about the
money. It's something far more important that concerns
me, Kira. I want Bella Terra to be much more than
simply a run-of-the-mill investment.' He grimaced, and
twitched a shoulder.

Kira turned back to the computer screen. He sounded
like the typical spoiled billionaire, bemoaning his idle
lifestyle.

'Ah, the curse of great wealth!' she muttered.

'I've told you—this isn't about money.' His retort was
swift and sure. 'You are a case in point—the first time
I looked across the valley from the Bella Terra villa I
assumed your cottage would be nothing but a horrible
reminder of everything I was trying to leave behind. And
yet when you let me get closer, I got a different angle
on your little garden and the homely touches inside. I
envy you, Kira.' He stopped abruptly and straightened
up. 'But maybe that was a case of giving you too much
information.'

She felt the exact opposite. 'Why in the world would
you envy me? I've got nothing, while you've got everything anyone could ever want!'

He modified his smile, and the angles of his fine face became acute. 'Is that what you think?'

Kira swung back to her screen. Tapping a few names over the keyboard, she accessed her file of planting suggestions for shady places. 'Pretty much.'

'Then I'll shut up. When I lived and worked on the streets, I spent too long listening to financiers and expats moaning. I was a tour guide, not an agony aunt—not that you would have believed it.' He put his coffee cup down beside hers.

'I'll bet you only guided the women!' Kira said with sly humour.

'That depended on where they wanted to be led,' he replied with an equally wicked grin. 'I gave a top-class service to everyone, whoever they were—every time. And that is how I got here.' He gestured around the IT suite of his impressive house. 'I saw that tour guides were always in demand, and they were invariably a rip-off. There was a gap in the market for a first-class service. I set myself up with a second-hand suit and the right attitude, and cleaned up. The sky was my limit, and it still is. My firm has branches all over the world, publishes travel guides—'

He stopped abruptly and frowned. 'And to think—I've had all that success, yet so little satisfaction.'

He leaned against the table beside the keyboard. Kira kept her eyes on her hands as she tapped over the keys.

'I want to be as happy in my houses as you are in your home, Kira,' he announced, and then chuckled. 'That's a tall order, but I believe you can give me answers to all my problems.'

Kira looked into his blue eyes and trembled to think

how much she wanted to do that. Attempting to sound crisp and businesslike, she said, 'Rest assured, I've never disappointed a client yet. If I work for you, I'll do my best to make all your dreams come true.'

CHAPTER SEVEN

KIRA blushed as she realised her words could so easily hold another meaning. She held her breath. Once again she had said exactly what she thought, and that was the problem. Her words were intended to be a promise to make all his desires for his properties come true. Instead, she might as well have told him her deepest feelings. He was watching her intently. Surely it was only a matter of time before she betrayed herself to him? She wanted to give this her best, but felt the need to hide her true emotions. As usual, work came to her rescue. She hit Return on the keyboard with all the force she would have liked to use on herself. The screen leapt into life again. Simulated raindrops falling on the surface of water became a display of plant photographs.

'Almost as beautiful as you,' Stefano said.

Kira thanked him tersely. His words reminded her of Chantal's patronising smile, and the way he could take his pick from all the lovely women in the world.

'I'll key in the details of your courtyard—its aspect, an estimate of the hours of sunshine it can expect—'

'There won't be much of that, I suspect.'

'I have a few ideas that can help,' Kira rallied. She always felt more confident when she could bring the subject around to the plants she loved. Dwelling on her own thoughts and feelings, and speculating on the way he might respond, made her uncomfortable. 'Some discreetly placed mirrors will bounce light into the shadowy places.'

'It sounds like the effect you have on me.'

He was leaning over her, only inches from where her fingers played on the keyboard. The subtle fragrance of his nearness was intoxicating. It was totally impossible to ignore. Kira felt her temperature rising as she logged all the details she had taken down so carefully. She tried to keep her eyes riveted on the screen, but within moments the effort was too much. They were constantly drawn back to Stefano's face. As though to prove he was able to ignore the effect he was having on her, he kept watching the rapidly developing images on the computer screen. Anticipation rose in Kira like a column of mercury. When she was almost at the point of screaming with need for him, he turned his clear blue eyes on her with a smile of sheer innocence.

'So you are confident you can give me what I want?'

His words were warm drops in a dipping pool of desire. He had chosen them with care. Knowing they were calculated for effect was the only thing that made it possible for Kira to resist him.

'While I'm working for you, that's all I'm interested in.'

Her voice was faint and strangely unsteady. Stefano continued to watch her, waiting for more signs that her resistance was weakening. Kira willed herself to return his gaze with equal candour, but she was powerless to stop a blush rippling over her skin. It was a firestorm of feeling. She needed distraction, and looked for it in a new computer image.

'Here's a mock-up of your quadrangle, with the rough shapes of some suggested plant groupings added.'

With one final flourish on the keyboard, she sat back and steadied her nerves with a sip of coffee. Stefano had drawn away slightly while she was typing, but now he leaned forward again. This time, Kira was strangely disappointed to find he was intent on the screen, rather than her.

'That's impressive.' He nodded slowly, his clear blue eyes flicking back and forth between the sidebars of text and the interactive graphics of the screen.

'It's only my first thoughts.' She basked in his approval, but tried not to show it. 'The final version will take a lot more work. And this is only the courtyard. I seem to remember you mentioned a roof garden?'

He nodded. 'There are some stark, flat areas resulting from repairs and building work done in the sixties. I like the idea of a hidden sanctuary that no one else knows about but me.'

'And me, as your designer,' Kira reminded him.

'The best secrets are those we are willing to share.'

Picking up on his enthusiasm, Kira smiled. 'Why don't we go up and inspect what you've got to offer?'

'I thought you'd never ask,' he said, already heading for the door.

Stefano's town house rambled over several floors. It was a warren of unexpected twists and turns. Kira always enjoyed the thrill of seeing how successful people ran their lives. She took in every detail when she visited their workplaces. This satellite branch of Albani International was no exception. Despite her solitary nature, whenever she took on a grand new job Kira spent her time idly wondering what she would tell her grandchildren. Today was different. There was nothing remotely idle about her thoughts. This wasn't just any grand house, owned by a faceless billionaire. It was where Stefano Albani lived. He worked and walked about here, and today he was strolling along beside her. The sensation was so powerful it had an immediate effect on all her dreams. Her fantasy grandchildren gained names, parents and inherited their grandfather's beautiful blue eyes and dark, dashing curls.

As Stefano piloted her along corridors scented by cream polish and fresh flower arrangements, she was torn. Admiring the modern, minimalist surroundings meant tearing her attention away from the gorgeous man at her side. He introduced her to everyone they passed by name. That was impressive. She wasn't quite so happy with the way he spoke to all the women in the same flirty fashion that set her own heart hammering.

'You're very quiet, Kira.' He smiled as they left the busy offices behind. Only the gentle burr of air conditioning followed them beyond a stained-glass door into his private quarters.

'I've been resisting the temptation to contradict you,' Kira said primly. 'You've asked everyone we met to welcome me onto your team. That ignores the tiny fact that I haven't actually agreed to sign your contract yet.'

Stefano's self-confidence shone through his reply. 'You will. You're an intelligent woman.'

His voice was as smooth as the glass elevator that took them up the final two storeys. Letting her out onto the roof, Stefano stood back to let her take in the whole breathtaking panorama. At this distance, the circling shoals of traffic sounded very faint and far away. The click of Kira's heels on the flat cement roof was loud, so she tried to make them sound efficient as well by striding straight over to the nearest parapet.

'This view is astonishing,' she breathed. 'You can see to the hills in almost every direction! We're so high I feel as though I could reach out and touch the dome of the cathedral. The light over the city is so beautiful. What do you suppose gives it that lovely golden glow?'

Stefano strolled to her side. Resting one hand against an ancient wall, he surveyed the scene with obvious pleasure. 'It is the Tuscan sun. It has mingled with the inspiration of poets, and matured over centuries.'

Pleased by the image, she turned to him with an unguarded smile, and found that he had switched his attention from the city to her.

'Do you think you can improve my situation?'

Kira considered her reply. She looked from the spectacular view to the dreary surroundings of his rooftop eyrie. Her mind went into overdrive. 'The beauty of beginning with nothing is that you can try whatever you like. Nobody could top an aerial view of Florence—but I can give you a better backdrop to it, Stefano. When you bring a beautiful woman like Chantal up here, she deserves something a lot better than bare cement and these pigeon prickles...' Patting the metal tangle that stopped birds perching on the parapet, Kira leaned out over the low wall. She was tempted to look straight down. It was a big mistake. Suddenly the events and emotions of the past two weeks rolled over her in a wave of dizziness.

'Ohh…'

She swayed for a terrifying moment, until Stefano seized her with his strong hands and pulled her back from the brink. Her eyes flew open, and she found herself looking up into his lean, intelligent face.

'It is never a good idea to stray too close to the edge,' he said brusquely.

His voice was wonderfully resonant. Kira felt so safe, but it frightened her.

'I—I know. I'm sorry, Stefano. I don't know what came over me.'

'This place can have a very strange effect.' His words were quiet and almost hesitant. They were in complete contrast to his iron grip as it crushed her against the solid security of his body.

'I'm beginning to realise that…' Kira's whisper rose between them like a dream.

'It makes me want to tell you again how beautiful you are, Kira,' he whispered.

She slowly shook her head. To her amazement, she felt Stefano contradict her with a definite nod. Neither of them moved for a long time. Then, in complete harmony, they came together in a kiss that made the world stand still.

After a long, long time, Stefano's lips left hers and he pressed his cheek hard against her hair.

'Come with me. Now,' he urged.

'I can't.'

'Why not?'

'I don't want to be hurt again.'

He stood back a little and looked down at her with a calm, forthright gaze. 'I would never do that.'

'I can't take that risk.' Desperation tore the words from her lips.

'I'm offering you nothing but good things, Kira. How can that bring you pain? Nothing lasts forever. We both know that. As long as we never forget it, there can be nothing but pleasure for us.'

He had been drawing her closer and closer. As his whisper died away, he kissed her with a power that held her long after he had drawn back from her lips.

'So let's enjoy that pleasure while we can....'

Wicked thoughts ran crazily through her mind. It's not as though he's married—no one will ever know, and if they do find out, it won't be like last time....

Her defences dissolved with the intensity of his smile. It was focused directly on her. There could be no resistance. Mirroring his expression, she nodded her head.

Stefano slid one arm around her shoulder and drew her back inside to the elevator. It took only seconds to reach his suite, but his hands were already dancing over the thin fabric of her clothes. He led her into the sophisticated setting of his private lounge. There he slid the jacket from her shoulders and flung it onto a glass-topped table.

'I know what you said about mixing business and pleasure, tesoro, but you would be the first to remind me you haven't actually signed my contract yet,' he murmured.

Kira veered between nervous tension and excitement at the thought of taking a leap into the unknown. For the first time in her life, temptation felt good. There was no need to wonder why. It was an opportunity to indulge in the fantasy that had been teasing her from the moment she first set eyes on him. A throaty chuckle rose up from somewhere deep within her.

'I think that's the perfect reason to make an exception.' Despite a tingle of fear, she wanted to find how far her body would go to quench this overriding fire for Stefano. She already sensed he would give her the ultimate in satisfaction. A strange combination of daring and desire unleashed all sorts of feelings deep in her body.

I know what I'm doing, she told herself. It'll be all right this time, because I'm watching for the danger signs. I can't resist him any more, but it doesn't matter because I don't want to try. I'm going into this with my eyes wide open. I'll enjoy Stefano while he satisfies my every need, but if he dares to try and get inside my heart, that's the end—no more.

From that moment on, there was no more thinking. She was aware of nothing but his touch on her arm and the movement of his body as he drew her into the silent sanctuary of his bedroom. The curtains were drawn against the afternoon sun. It was as cool and shadowy as an oasis at dusk, lit only by a narrow strip where the floor-length curtains were not quite fully closed. A tiny fragment of goose down spiralled upwards in the single shaft of sunlight. It looks as light as my heart feels, Kira thought. It was the last thing she remembered before a surge of need carried away all her inhibitions.

He was more gentle than even her fantasies had promised. His fingertips had a delicacy of touch that sent shivers of delight dancing over her skin. When his cheek brushed her face the roughness of his incipient stubble released a little cry of desire from her lips. It no longer mattered that he had travelled this route with one girl or a thousand. While she was in his arms, Kira felt like the only woman in the world. As the silk and lace of her slip slithered away, she was filled with the exuberance of being. Standing in a pool of sunlight beneath the warm appreciation of Stefano's haunting gaze, she felt the life force thunder through her body. This was where she wanted to be, now and forever.

'Carissima mia,' he breathed in a way that drew Kira's whole attention right back to him.

With a flutter of delight she saw a subtle change come over him. It wasn't so much a new look in his eyes, as the sudden loss of something she had not wanted to acknowledge before. Playful amusement no longer danced in his expression. Stefano was a changed man. For once he was not the flippant lover of thousands. All his attention was devoted to her and her alone.

'You don't mean that,' she murmured, while hoping with all her heart that he did.

'Would you like to put me to the test?' his voice rasped through the drowsy silence. It was thick with an emotion she had never heard from him before. He took one, two steps across the soft rug. Now they were so close, she could feel the warmth of desire radiating from him. His heat transformed her. With a moan of anticipation, her head fell back.

'You are so lovely.'

His voice was a whisper. Kira felt fingertips dance lightly over her face, and then dive into the rippling luxuriance of her coppery hair. His kiss was a long, thoughtful expression of delight. Pressing his forehead against hers, he slid his arms around her body, drawing it close. 'I've said that so many times, to so many different girls, but this is the first time it has been from the core of my being, mia tesoro.'

Kira opened her eyes. Another transformation swept over his face, and with delight she put her hand up to touch the uncharacteristic colour flushing his cheeks. He was holding her with a possessive strength as they sank into the yielding luxury of his bed. Stefano kissed his way down the curve of her neck, before lifting her arm to tease the delicate skin beneath. His lips pleasured her breasts and belly, encouraging her to stretch out languorously across his silken sheets. It was such a lovely, leisurely feeling that when he pulled away from her she tried to follow him, jealous of every second he spent away from her arms.

Stefano had no intention of disappointing her. He had only knelt up to strip off his clothes and give her the full benefit of his magnificent body.

'I want to feel my naked skin against yours.'

His demand was husky but his movements were smooth and unhurried. Watching the relish in his beautiful eyes as he twined his lithe golden limbs around hers was the most wonderful aphrodisiac. As his body glided over and around hers, she floated in the clear blue of his admiring gaze. His hands and lips brought her to the peak of pleasure, time after time, and he left no room in her mind for any doubts. She was his, and she could not get enough of him. Only when she was almost faint from this glorious pleasure overload did he turn to his own satisfaction. With a wild cry his body convulsed in the sheer pleasure of orgasm.

The physical release was absolute, but a new kind of torment was about to begin. Kira had never known her mind and body meld in such a way, but it could not last.

As Stefano enfolded her gently in his arms, she knew things could never be the same between them.

'That was beyond even what I had hoped for,' he murmured.

As he drifted off to sleep, he took Kira's sense of proportion with him. She lay in the gloom, unable to put her fears into words and unwilling to wake him. She had never been in exactly this situation before, but something about it was frighteningly familiar. Her mind reeled back the years to her only other intimate encounter. She had been swept off her feet then, too. Before, during and after sex she had been suspended in a make-believe world which almost instantly unravelled. Her illusions vanished with the cold light of an Oxford morning. The tutor she once idolised had only used her to relieve his midlife crisis. How long would it be before the younger, more virile Stefano wrecked her dreams in a similar way?

She lay awake through all the long dark hours of the night. She knew exactly how this would end. The pain and humiliation were all too familiar. Listening to Stefano's soft, regular breathing as he slept, it was agonising to think he would start taking her for granted from the moment he woke. The infatuation she felt would not survive the death of his sweet words and sensuous touch. She couldn't bear to think he would never look at her in the same way again. What had she done? She had ruined all her own dreams by fulfilling his desires. From the moment she succumbed to his charm, the doomsday clock began marking time on their relationship.

She turned her head. Outside, dawn was breaking. She looked back at him. In sleep, his brow was smooth and untroubled. His finely carved features were heart-breakingly handsome. Such a man would never stay with someone like her. She could not endure the thought of never seeing him again, but what was the alternative? If she didn't run away now, he would dump her. It was as simple as that.

As the sun crept above the distant rim of hills she agonised over what she should do. If she bolted now, she would lose everything—Stefano's respect, any chance for another blissful coupling and all those wonderful opportunities he had promised her. Work seemed a million miles away when she was still being cradled in his arms, but she could not live without it. Her job was her reality. The rhythm and routine of it endured, although everything around her might be falling apart. Stefano's starry list of contacts could ensure the survival of her business.

It took a long time, but Kira had plenty of experience in teasing out the good points of a bad situation. Eventually, she worked out a restless compromise. While Stefano was busy in Florence, she would make sure she was working on his Bella Terra estate. When he retreated to his country hideaway, she would turn her attention to his town house. That way, accepting his offer of a contract would give her the excuse to keep in touch while staying out of his hands.

Holding onto that thought like a lucky charm, Kira eased her way out of bed and headed for the bathroom. Stepping into the shower, she tried to blast away all her regrets. It was impossible. She couldn't have any. Then, to compound her sin, she saw the bathroom door open. Stefano walked in.

He was naked, and joined her in the shower as though

it was the most natural thing in the world. Already shamed by her complete lack of guilt, Kira squeaked and tried to cover herself with her hands. It didn't impress him for a second.

'There isn't a single centimetre of your body that I haven't admired and kissed, *cara*,' he said as the water coursed over him.

'Stefano, this has got to stop,' Kira announced, with as much force as she could against the warm, relaxing water and the tempting sight of his naked body.

'Of course. But not for a little while.' His voice fell as softly as the water.

Squeezing shower gel over his hands, he stroked it expertly over her shoulders and back. The warmth of him in the confined space of the shower cubicle intensified the lemony fragrance of the bubbles he caressed across her skin. Despite her determination not to weaken, Kira could not resist. She closed her eyes, and let her head fall back as he worshipped her body with hands and lips. As they stood beneath the powering torrent of hot water, she felt the urgency of his desire match hers. She moved in close to the sheltering power of his body, pressing herself eagerly against the growing ridge of his manhood. Reaching around, he cupped her bottom in his hands and lifted her off the ground. Kira instinctively twined her legs around his waist. He entered her with a guttural sigh of satisfaction that echoed her own cry of need. Water coursed over their naked bodies as they coupled with a fierce, animal urgency. Kira's orgasm clenched him with a grip as hard as iron, and with a gasp he stopped the water and carried her out of the cubicle. Pulling all the towels from the hot rail, he made a soft nest on the marble floor and settled her down in it.

'Now I know exactly how to please you, I can delay my own pleasure for as long as I like.' Testosterone lowered his voice and made his smile wolflike.

Kira moaned with anticipation as his mouth dipped to nibble one nipple while the pads of his thumb and index finger rolled the other into a hard peak of anticipation. She lost count of the number of times he sent her sweeping over the edge. When she was sure her body could take no more she opened her mouth to beg him to stop, but he anticipated her cry.

'Now it's my turn,' he growled.

Stefano woke her with a kiss. Kira opened her eyes and realised that at some stage they had left the bathroom and moved on, in more ways than one. Stefano was standing beside the bed. He was fully dressed and ready for work. Kira smelled hot coffee and warm pastry, and saw he was holding a tray. She struggled to sit up, the sheet slipping away from her nakedness again. His business suit was beautifully cut, but could not conceal the sudden rise of his manhood as he looked down on her appreciatively.

She looked from him to the breakfast tray. It was set for one.

'Are you leaving, Stefano?'

He placed the tray on her lap. It was complete with fruit, cappuccino and brioche, fresh from his kitchens. Kira gazed at the beautiful display in wonder.

'I'm afraid I must.'

'Two weeks ago, I stopped you coming upstairs in my own home. Now I'm in your bed,' she said faintly. Kira couldn't believe her luck, but wasn't sure whether it would turn out to be the bad kind of fortune, or the good. A long shadow was lowering over the best, most exciting job prospect she had ever been offered. Any woman would be a fool to trust such a dedicated ladies' man. She would be doubly stupid: mixing work and a man had derailed her life once already. It would take a special sort of idiot to fall into that trap a second time. Kira was determined to stay independent. And yet, to resist such an opportunity…

There wasn't much time to decide. Stefano was already heading towards the door.

'I must go. Multi-billion-dollar enterprises don't run themselves, you know.' He smiled at her. 'Take your time to consider my contract, and let me know what you decide. If you make the sensible choice, I'll send a car to collect you later today—I want to take you to Silver Island.'

Kira made a snap decision. 'There's no need. I've made up my mind—I'll sign it.'

Stefano paused, one hand on the door frame. Genuine pleasure, but no real surprise, lit his eyes for a moment. 'I am glad. We have a lot in common, Kira.'

At his reminder of what they had so spectacularly shared, nervous defiance flared in Kira again. 'I can't always be relied on to do exactly as anyone says, Stefano, and once I'm working for you we can't carry on…'

He nodded, and his bright blue eyes became serious. 'Of course. You are your own woman…apart from those moments when I make you mine. So, until later…'

He reached over and kissed her hard, driving all thoughts of rebellion from her mind and leaving her gasping. When she drew back she only just stopped herself reaching for him again. Stefano gave her a look that made her blush. It said he knew exactly what she was feeling. A moment later, he was gone.

CHAPTER EIGHT

KIRA gazed after him, hardly able to believe what had happened. It was madness, she told herself over and over again. It didn't make a shred of difference. All she could think about was the look in Stefano's eyes as he left. His eyes had been dark and full of longing. The memory worked away at her, slowly chipping out a special place for him in her stony heart. Her ill-fated liaison with the lecturer who seduced her had never been anything like this. Hugh Taylor had lied and schemed to get her—and other women—into bed.

Stefano isn't like that, she thought, and then told herself the only difference was his honesty. She had thought of him as Stefano the Seducer before she met him, and that may be true, but at least he was truthful about it. He was quite happy to be the man of her dreams, as long as she woke up afterwards. He never made any pretence at being in this for the long haul. He was out for what he could get, but on their first night together, so was she. Once he sated her desires, Kira delighted in what she could give him.

It had never been like that with Hugh. She had been so upset by the whole business she had abandoned her university course and turned away from academic life

altogether. Making love with Stefano made her think
and feel in totally new ways. This wasn't some hole-
in-the-corner affair. It was an awakening, and one she
could dream of experiencing with him again.

She had total recall of every single second she spent
with Stefano. It was all so special. She couldn't stop
smiling. It had felt so perfect....

Suddenly a shiver ran over her skin. Her smile vanished. The spectre of her past reached out a cold bony
finger and tapped her on the shoulder. She had known
Stefano for only a few hours, yet her feelings had a cast-
iron certainty about them. It made her look deep into her
heart. She had never felt this way about Hugh. Never.
The firework of that brief infatuation with her tutor had
been hot and dangerous, but it had never reached this
pitch of perfection. She ached for Stefano with a longing that scared her. He was bound to be as faithless as
Hugh. How could she risk her heart and peace of mind
again?

The answer was simple.

Because it is Stefano, she told herself, and this time
I'm the one in control of the relationship. I won't sac-
rifice the most exciting job I've ever been offered because I'm afraid of pain. I'll throw my heart and soul
into my projects for him. That will satisfy us both, she
thought.

When the maid arrived, she found Kira still sitting
where Stefano had left her. She was gazing over the
rooftops of Florence, lost in thought. Her conscience
might be clear, but her eyes were clouded.

Stefano leaned back in his chauffeur-driven Mercedes
and breathed a long sigh of contentment. He was still
relishing the details of his night of pleasure with Kira.

Soon he would be relaxing on Silver Island with the world's most passionate woman. When they eventually returned to Italy, the Bella Terra villa would be ready for him to move in. Life did not get any better than this.

He felt his brow pleat at the thought of going back to the office. The contrast between these past carefree hours and the urban jungle could not have been more marked. A scowl was as necessary a part of his office uniform as a designer suit and a Rolex. All his working life Stefano had been perfecting that image. Now he had the kingdom to go with it. Everything should have been worthwhile, at last. Today, he had it all—or so everyone kept telling him.

The creases accentuated his dark, beautifully arched brows. Deep in thought, he braced himself for re-entry into the business world of concrete and cut-throats. That was his domain during the working day. Nothing was ever allowed to distract him from it.

Then a faint, feminine perfume drifted through his limousine. He looked around. He had no idea where the scent could be coming from, until inspiration struck. Turning up the lapel of his jacket, he sniffed it appreciatively. He had leaned so close to Kira when he kissed her awake, some of her delicious fragrance had attached itself to his clothes. It brought back all those soft, sweet memories of the night he had spent with his lady of the flowers.

For a split second his frown disappeared again, and he smiled.

Kira's new project was the only thing that could stop her thinking about Stefano. Even that did not work for long. She was continually drawn back by the memory of his whispers through their one unforgettable night together. As she walked along the corridors of his big old town house, she let her thoughts dawdle deliciously over him and his body.

But the moment she crossed any threshold, work took first place again. Daydreams were put on hold until she had noted down a room's aspects and angles of light. It was only as she left that she took a moment to look back and appreciate it. The whole building, every nook and cranny, was filled with faded splendour. All the modern art and electronic offices could not hide its beauty. Every passage was full of interest. The rooms were absorbing. She really relished the chance to choose plants to soften and beautify the balconies and public areas. Most of all she wanted to see Stefano's pleasure—in her work, and in her.

As she was dreaming along an upper corridor, her mobile began to dance.

'Stefano!' To her shame, she almost dropped the phone.

'I never thought one single word could be charged with so much guilt,' he lilted. 'Don't say I caught you with your hand in a cookie jar?'

'No...no, I was busy thinking about something, that's all,' she muttered, her voice indistinct with embarrassment. She had been thinking about him, naked, and spreadeagled across her bed. 'You disturbed me when I was working,' she countered more sharply, as she managed to bring herself back to reality. There was much more truth in her words than he could ever imagine!

'I'm glad to hear you're taking things so seriously. Clearly, this will be a really good relationship—a really good *working* relationship,' he corrected himself carefully.

In spite of her misgivings, Kira blossomed under the warmth of his voice and his small slip-up. It felt as though she grew several inches. Not for the first time, she found that smiling was compulsory whenever Stefano was involved. She couldn't help herself, especially when she heard what he said next.

'Go home and throw a few things into a suitcase. A car will be round to collect you in a couple of hours' time, and take you to the airport,' he announced in a voice that made her tingle with anticipation. 'I'm taking you to see phase two of your commission to landscape my properties.'

The next few hours passed by in a blur. Kira was whisked to the airport and straight onto Stefano's private plane. He met her at the top of the steps and kissed her hand in greeting. She hesitated, not knowing how he wanted to play this reunion. His lips still pressing against her fingers, he gazed at her. The look in his blue eyes was watchful rather than seductive.

'Kira…' He made her name sound so beautiful she blushed. 'Welcome. In a few hours you'll see an entirely new kind of paradise.'

He seemed to be waiting for her reaction, so he could fine-tune his own. Kira decided to play it cool, although the mere sight of him threatened to send her temperature off the scale. She looked around appreciatively. The jet was new and smelled of luxury. Inside, the spacious cabin was an extension of his elegant furnished suite in Florence. It was thickly carpeted, and softly upholstered with linens and silks.

'Paradise? I think I've already arrived,' she breathed, wide-eyed.

* * *

Their trip to Silver Island was smooth and fast. Anything Kira could possibly want was to hand. There was a selection of magazines, several shelves of contemporary and classic novels, but she took her lead from Stefano. After his watchful greeting, he turned to his work. Surrounded by papers, he was riveted to his computer screen. Kira was almost relieved. She had packed her laptop case with plenty of work, and cautiously picked a workstation on the other side of the aeroplane. It kept her within reach, while maintaining the privacy she usually guarded so fiercely.

Unfortunately, it no longer felt quite so natural to keep her distance from him. Many times during the flight she felt her eyes drawn across the cabin to where he sat. To glance at him openly was to run the risk he might start a conversation. Kira had no idea what she could to say to him, outside the subjects of bed and the plans for his properties. She wasn't sure words would come easily on those subjects, either. With relief, she fell back on her plans for the Florence town house and its roof garden. Soon she was lost in her imagination, but it was still impossible to forget Stefano's presence. Every few moments a strange feeling crept over her, as though she was being bathed in a warm glow. The first few times it happened, she glanced up at him. He was always hard at work. With a shrug, she would turn back to her work, puzzled. It was odd. She could practically feel his eyes on her, but each time she checked he was gazing impassively at his paperwork.

Finally, the pilot announced that Silver Island was coming into view over the starboard wing. Kira instantly looked out of the window. A scatter of green islands rose softly from a sea that was almost as tranquil as Stefano's eyes.

'Oh, I've never seen anything so lovely!' she gasped.

'I have,' Stefano said quietly.

Kira looked over her shoulder, ready to make room for him if he joined her for a view from the window. He never moved. Instead, he sat back in his seat, watching her with a steady gaze.

'And if you think that is beautiful,' he murmured, 'wait until you are framed by orchids, set against a tropical moon and a sky scattered with stars.'

They flew in to a private airstrip. Unlike the sun trap of the Bella Terra estate, this land was cooled by sea breezes. The atmosphere was as clear as crystal. As she stepped down from the plane Kira stretched her arms up to the sun and revelled in the sharp salty tang in the air.

'This is wonderful,' she breathed, but the dream was just beginning. A car swept up to take them to a nearby quay. There, brightly painted fishing boats bobbed alongside the sun-warmed boardwalk, but Stefano led her towards a very different craft. Handing her down into a sleek black-and-gold speedboat, he took the controls and headed out towards a blue-green cloud low on the horizon.

'This is where I thought to make my base, until I discovered the Bella Terra estate,' he told her as the speedboat skipped across the clear blue sea like a flying fish. Kira watched indistinct shapes in the distance become a necklace of islands set in the warm, shallow sea. High, forested mountains rose up from shallow shelving beaches of flawless white sand. As they ran into the shallows, she saw the tension ease from Stefano's face once more. Boys playing football on the beach raced to greet them. As Stefano handed over the mooring rope, Kira was seized by a mad impulse. By the time he moved to help her from the boat she had slipped off her sandals and jumped barefoot into the water.

'Careful, the surf runs fast here!' Stefano called, but his warning was too late.

Dizzy with travel and excitement, Kira was pulled in two directions at once. Her feet went from under her and she promptly sat down in two feet of surging water. Stefano reached down and hauled her up. She surfaced, spluttering, to roars of laughter from the beach footballers.

'Are you all right?' Stefano's concern was obvious, but Kira was laughing as hard as anyone.

'It's wonderful!' She giggled, pushing her drenched hair back from her face. Her skirt was sodden, and wrapped itself in clinging folds around her slender legs.

'Take a seat and catch your breath.' He took her towards the treeline, where coconut palms draped cool shadows out over the sand. Kira sat down thankfully on a perfectly placed trunk. Instantly, a waiter appeared at her side. He was holding a tray with two tall glasses of passion-fruit cocktail, clinking with ice.

'This is heaven!' she gasped. Stefano laughed.

'Not yet, but it will be. I've gathered a world-class team to create an island paradise, and you're here to see how it can be made still more stunning.'

Kira took a long, slow sip of her drink. 'It'll be a challenge—' she smiled mischievously '—but I'm sure I'll think of something.'

'There's no hurry,' he said softly. 'No hurry at all. It's been a long flight. Shall I show you where you can freshen up?'

Kira bit her lip. She had spent the night with Stefano. There could be no secrets between them now, but that was what made her afraid. He was about to lead her to his suite. She wasn't ready for that and knew she should refuse, yet at the same it was everything she wanted. Stefano barely seemed to notice.

'I've had one of the guest suites made ready for you,' he said, taking her hand and leading her across the white, warm sand. Her sigh was a strange mixture of relief and disappointment, and he looked back with a laugh.

'Did you think I'd forget what you told me? You said there would be no repeat of our passionate night once you had signed my contract. I don't intend to blur the line between employer and employee.'

'Thank goodness for that,' Kira said determinedly, but with a heart that had suddenly plummeted. *Fool!* she berated herself. *Don't mistake his flirtation for serious intentions. It's good that he wants to keep this businesslike.* Tell herself what she would, however, the idea that she might never go to bed with Stefano again made her feel as though she'd lost something utterly precious. Caught up in her thoughts, she nearly missed his next words.

'Although I like to keep my staff happy,' he went on, and suddenly his eyes lit up with a dangerous spark. 'So I always make a special effort for new arrivals. That's why I'm inviting you to dinner at my apartment this evening.'

He moved closer. Kira felt it with every heartbeat. If

he was trying to test her, she was equal to it. 'Like you, I always mean what I say, Stefano.'

His eyes twinkled in the dancing sunlight. 'Fine. I wanted to see if you had changed your mind, that's all.'

With a wolfish smile he lifted her chin with his hand. She had been remembering his touch all day, but her memory was nowhere near as powerful as the real thing. His skin glided over hers like a kiss of fire, drawing a gasp from her lips.

'Second chances make life worth living, don't you think?'

His voice ended in a whisper of longing. Enfolding her in the curve of his arm, he drew her the last few inches towards his body. His kiss was a long, slow promise of all the things Kira knew he was so brilliant at. She could not help but respond. She was aware of all the dangers, but they were nothing when matched against his powers of seduction. Knowing she should pull back, she forced herself to do it.

At her first hesitation he let her go. His hands drifted regretfully from her body. She took a step back from him, struggling to catch her breath. Her common sense was marginally easier to manage.

'Last night was a mistake. One of those should be enough for both of us.'

His touch slid down her back, lingered around her ribs and then fell away. Pushing his hands deep into his pockets, he shrugged.

'I know—' he gave her an irrepressible smile '—but you surely can't blame me for trying?'

'I've told you. Now I'm officially on your payroll,

there can be nothing between us. I'm only interested in doing the best I can for you.'

He cocked his head on one side and regarded her with the keen look of a bush robin. 'Ah, but in what way?'

'You're my employer, nothing more,' Kira said firmly, desperately in need of the reminder. She had managed to keep her emotions out of it—until now. She could feel herself sliding out of control. Equally determined to call her bluff, Stefano wasn't about to give her a second chance to back down.

'Okay. If that's how you feel, follow me, and I shall show you to your room.'

He was already walking away. Kira was drawn along in his wake, trying to catch up.

'Isn't it lovely? Silver Island is the ideal refuge for me—and anyone I choose to invite here.'

Those last words were thrown casually over his shoulder as he walked into the treeline. Kira followed him. She caught him up as he breasted a little rise where palms gave way to lush, leafy shrubs. This oasis of cool shade was the perfect place for a collection of freshly whitewashed buildings. Each was roofed with yellow ochre tiles, patterned with age.

'That's my headquarters.' Stefano pointed out the largest building as they crossed a clearing. 'Like all my properties, the first thing I do is bring in office staff, so I can keep my finger on the pulse of business, day and night.'

Kira laughed at the picture he painted.

'It's no wonder you never feel at home! You make everywhere into an extension of your office.'

Stefano frowned and did not reply. They drew closer to the buildings. As they crossed the pine- and balsam-scented clearing, a cloud of brightly coloured parakeets exploded into the air from the eaves of an apartment building. It was twice the size of La Ritirata. Unlike Kira's ancient little home, its roof was supported by all the walls in all the right places. She was instantly impressed. As Stefano showed her up the steps of her temporary home, she was already wondering what design ideas she could take back with her.

'Well? What do you think?'

Kira had been too wrapped up in her own thoughts to realise Stefano was interested in her opinion. When she jumped at his light touch on her waist, he dropped his hand and stepped back. Hurriedly, she went in to discover her apartment's air-conditioned luxury—and stopped dead.

'It's amazing!' she breathed, and it was true. Her luggage stood in the centre of a large, cool room. There were big, squashy chairs and a matching settee for loafing. The floor covering was thick and plush. Beautiful art stood on every shelf, while woven hangings added splashes of colour against the sparkling white walls. Everything was brand new—and it was all oddly soulless, as though the wraps had been taken off this apartment especially for her.

'Am I your only guest, Stefano?'

'At the moment, yes.' He strolled over to where a reclining nude sculpted from rich red wood stood on a side table. Drawing his fingers over its glowing flanks, he gazed at her thoughtfully. 'At least, you're the first to stay in this particular building.'

Kira didn't say anything. Instead, she let him show her around the bland and beautiful apartment. Everything was absolutely right, from the wall hangings to the ethnic rugs and the huge gold-and-marble bathroom.

'I think it's wonderful,' Kira said as she strolled into her new bedroom. A genuine Victorian bed stood at its heart. The pillows and thick, soft mattress looked so inviting—but to her embarrassment her first thoughts at the sight of such a bed were certainly not of sleep.

'I'm impressed you haven't followed me in here,' she said airily.

Her words provoked a reaction in him, but too late she discovered it wasn't the one she wanted.

'You said you wanted me to stop all that,' he drawled, leaning against the door frame.

With a pang, she turned to face him. Her first rebuke had worked better than she expected. One look at his beautiful face and she knew he could see through her flinty manner to the real, pulsating woman within. She flushed with shame as he continued to watch her, his gaze feeling heavy as a caress on her skin.

'From now on,' he said softly, 'you're the one who makes the decisions. For example, whether you want to have dinner with me this evening at eight o'clock is entirely up to you.'

It was a statement, not a question. Before he finished speaking he pushed himself upright and strolled away through her apartment.

Stefano caught himself smiling as he headed for his own bungalow. That was a surprise. He had known Kira was a passionate woman beneath her reserve, but he hadn't expected such untapped depths of sensuality. She had been so determined not to fall for his charm that usually he would have looked elsewhere without a second thought, but she was different. Her hands put a stop to their kiss on the beach, but her lips told a different story. Stefano knew women and Kira Banks was definitely a girl worth waiting for. She would make such a change from the extrovert capers of his usual women. She needed much more careful handling, and Stefano knew he was the ideal man to conquer her fears. A few days of his company, together with the allure of this tropical island, would slowly melt her English reserve.

Like a stalking leopard, Stefano settled down for a long wait.

Kira watched him walk away. He never once looked back, although something told her he knew very well that her eyes were on him. She stayed motionless, until he disappeared inside his bungalow and closed the door. It was only then she took refuge inside her own rooms.

Leaning back against the closed door, she looked around. This place was paradise. A wand of fragrant orchids peeped over the nearest windowsill. Outside, the parakeets returned, tumbling over the eaves and squawking with delight. Silver Island had everything— including the only man she could ever want. This should be the project from heaven, and more holiday than work. Yet Kira already felt stressed. She might as well have been back in England, trying to sort out her stepparents' chaotic finances.

She knew she should ignore Stefano's invitation to dinner. Her willpower would be under pressure from the moment she crossed his threshold.

Somehow, that didn't feel like such a terrible threat any more. A small smile flitted across her face. When

Stefano wasn't with her, she missed him. That was a totally alien experience for Kira. It made her feel unsure of herself. She didn't like it, but she did like Stefano—in a way that encouraged all sorts of outrageous thoughts.

She was having a particularly wild idea right now. Any truly independent, intelligent person ought to be able to accept his invitation to dinner. She had come a long way over the past couple of years. She was a successful businesswoman. A perfectly respectable dinner with a man she fancied was exactly the treat she deserved for landing such a lucrative contract. It would also be an opportunity to put herself to the test. If she succeeded in resisting Stefano this evening, she would be unstoppable. There would be no limit to what she could achieve, if only she could show her new boss that not every woman would roll over and beg for his body straight away.

If she failed, the worst that could happen was that he would ravish her senseless. Her heart and mind would never be in danger. They were safely locked away, somewhere Stefano would never be allowed to find them.

Kira felt she couldn't lose.

CHAPTER NINE

ONE long, luxurious bath later, Kira slipped into the single evening dress she had packed. It was a silky little emerald number she had worn for the most recent Chelsea gala night.

I'll show Stefano that when it comes to his charms, I can be chilled steel. I can resist him, she told herself a hundred times.

The mirror told a different story. Her eyes were dark with arousal. The tip of her tongue rested against the glossy cushion of her lower lip as she pinned her mane of auburn hair up into a sophisticated coil. The sight made her smile. She looked good, and knew it. Loose tendrils danced over the creamy curves of her neck and shoulders. Her dress was a sumptuous slither of sequinned silk. Its opulent shade of green complemented the rich tawny of her hair. With every movement it shimmered like the sea.

As she twirled and swirled in front of the full-length mirror, Kira went on deceiving herself. Instead of trying to put Stefano off by dressing like a drudge, she would make this evening still more of a challenge by making herself irresistible. Then, when he tried to seduce her and failed, her triumph would be complete. After all, when we met I was only dressed in dusty jeans and look what happened then! It's not the clothes he should be interested in, but what is inside them, she told herself, managing to limit her self-delusion right at the end. There was absolutely no point in imagining he was only interested in her brain. To her horror, the reflection looking back from the glass smiled instead of frowned. Stefano Albani was all man. He had proved it to her any number of times during their fantastic night together.

She checked her appearance again. Her smile faltered, and then returned with added self-assurance. She loved this dress, and for once the torture of a social occasion was going to be sweet, sweet, sweet.

She added one last finishing touch. It was truly spectacular. With her first impressive pay cheque, Kira had spoiled herself with a real diamond necklace. It contained the smallest stones in captivity, brilliantly cut and cleverly set to make them look larger. Tiny they might be, but she was really proud of her necklace. It didn't matter to her that she never went anywhere she could wear it. That wasn't the point. It was beautiful, and it was hers.

She laid the galaxy of tiny stars against her skin and fastened the catch. Then she took the matching earrings from their royal-blue velvet bed. It had taken her a further two years of careful saving to add them to her collection, and this was the first time they had been out of the box. Finally, glittering like moonlight on the sea, she set off on the nerve-racking walk to Stefano's bungalow.

Her nerves were tuned to a high C of tension by the time she reached his apartment. They weren't helped by movement sensors switching on a battery of security lights. Startled by the sudden blaze, a deer shot away through the undergrowth. It leapt like her heart as it dived into cover. That close shave did nothing for Kira's nerves. Feeling like a prisoner on the run under all the lights, she started up the front steps. Raising her hand, she knocked hesitantly. Five…ten…fifteen seconds passed with no reply. Then she noticed the bell. The bungalow was so large, the chances were that Stefano hadn't heard her nervous tapping. She leaned on the bell, and heard it echoing through the building beyond. He must have heard it, but it still felt an awfully long time passed between pressing the button and seeing the bungalow door open.

'Kira.'

Stefano loomed in the doorway, dressed in an immaculate white shirt and dark trousers. He looked magnificent, but it was his expression that snatched her breath away. He was looking at her with the same illicit pleasure she had seen in her reflection only a few moments before. 'You look incredible.'

'Thank you!' she said breathlessly, relying on the glittering diamonds, sequins, lipgloss and nail polish to speak for her. It was a risky venture. There was a fine line between untouchable beauty and come-hither.

He stepped back from the door with an inviting gesture. 'Come in and make yourself comfortable.'

Kira followed him into the bungalow. The building smelled of new money and even newer paint. It was as tasteful as her own apartment, and just as soulless.

'I've given most of my staff the evening off.'

Kira stared at him. He returned her look with one that danced with silent amusement.

Escape was still not impossible. She could have reached out and touched the door from where she was standing. All it needed was a quick goodnight. She could make some excuse and slip out into the safety of darkness, beyond the security lighting.

She didn't do any of those things. Instead, she looked around. Rather than cowering by the door, she began to unfold like a flower. After all, she told herself, there's no triumph in running away. She had accepted Stefano's invitation. If she took up the challenge of treating him like a trustworthy employer rather than a casual lover, that was even better.

Stefano began moving around the room with careful deliberation. Under Kira's gaze, he shook sofa cushions and dragged scattered magazines into a pile.

'Now you've had time to settle into your own apartment, why don't you have a look around here, and tell me what you think?' he asked her as he prowled around.

'I think you have a beautiful house, on a lovely island. The peace and quiet here make it almost as perfect as the Bella Terra valley,' she said simply.

'Almost?' Stefano asked.

Kira didn't answer him. The large main room of his apartment had been painted pale ochre, with the woodwork a slightly lighter shade. It was sparsely furnished, with polished boards rather than carpet on the floor. They gave it a rather hollow feeling. The whole atmosphere was light and bright rather than warm and welcoming. It echoed the impersonal touch that seemed to follow Stefano around, but she didn't know how to explain it to him. Instead, she went to investigate two long leather couches and a beautiful large glass coffee table while he headed for the sound system.

'Make yourself comfortable while I set things in motion. We're dining on the mainland, so I'll alert the launch.' He walked towards the nearest telephone.

'Oh…I thought we'd be eating here?' Kira could not keep the disappointment from her voice. 'Leaving this paradise and plunging back into the chaos of city life doesn't appeal in the slightest.'

Stefano had been studying one of his works of art with a critical eye. When she said that, he stopped and looked straight at her instead. A slow smile spread across his face 'Squisita! You are an unusual woman, Kira. Not everyone would choose a simple dinner rather than air-conditioned luxury.'

'Well, I would,' said Kira firmly. 'You are so lucky, being able to escape from everyone and everything whenever you like.'

His art collection forgotten, Stefano's attention was now firmly riveted on Kira. One hand in his pocket he strolled towards her, his eyes intent on her face.

'Is that what you think?'

Kira looked askance. 'Why would I say something I didn't mean?'

'You'd be surprised how many people do. All of the women I speak to, as a matter of fact. With one notable exception.' He inclined his head to her, interest very obvious in his beautiful eyes.

'That's what living does for you.' Kira was hardly aware of what she was saying. Only one thing mattered, and that was the lovely warm feeling that came from basking in his appreciation. 'It's easy to forget what life is actually about.'

'And what do you think that is?' He was looking at

her with intensity and his expression demanded nothing less than the absolute truth.

'I'd love to be able to say home and family, but I've only got experience of half that equation. I've got the home. It's better than I ever dreamed it would be, but I've never known what a happy family feels like. My idea of what it must be like is hopelessly romantic. Please shoot all my delusions down in flames by telling me your Italian family background is full of fights and bad feeling, and not a bit like the cheerful stereotype!' Kira tried to joke past the pain, but she wasn't the only one with issues. For the first time in heart-stopping minutes, Stefano avoided her eyes. It was a painful reminder that she might not be the only person in the world hiding inner turmoil.

Walking over to the fully stocked bar that stood in a far corner of the room, he spooned ice cubes into two tall glasses. 'What would you like?'

To take back the last thing I said, Kira thought, wishing she hadn't rattled on so cheerfully. 'I'll have a St Clement's, please,' she muttered.

As a distraction, it worked perfectly. Stefano left the bar and stepped through a pair of French doors. Kira watched him reach out and select the ripest fruit from big old citrus trees shading the veranda. When he returned, so did his smile. In one hand he held a spray of polished, dark green leaves. Nestling at their heart was a cluster of waxy white blossoms and purple-stained buds. He held it out to her gallantly.

'This is for you, to make up for the bouquet that would have been waiting for you at the restaurant in town.'

'Thank you!' she whispered, glowing with pleasure.

The heavy, sweet fragrance stole through the warm evening air between them. 'It's lovely!'

'Then it is exactly the right gift for you,' he said quietly, moving in still closer. 'Let me see how it can be fixed…'

'No!' Kira leapt back in alarm. It was already hard enough keeping him at arm's length. When he lavished her with flowers and soft words, it was impossible. 'I mean, no, thank you. The perfume is so powerful I'd rather have them in a vase on the table.' *And I can pretend to be looking at them, when I'm really looking at you!* The words raced desperately through her mind as she watched him walk back to the bar. He halved all the fruit and extracted the juice with powerful but deft movements. Then he presented her with a perfect cocktail.

'That's really impressive. You handled that knife like a professional.'

'Call it the legacy of a wasted youth,' he said, mixing himself the driest of dry martinis.

'I know all about that,' she said with a shiver as the ice rattled enticingly in her glass.

Stefano's shoulders visibly relaxed, as though he had ordered them to. Until that moment Kira had assumed he was always perfectly at ease. Now she knew better. The change in him was noticeable. The mask was back in place.

'I doubt that very much, but we can discuss it over dinner. What would you like? Name it, and my chef will make it for you.'

He must have been through this routine with a thousand women. Kira heard the ring of fine crystal echoing again across the glade from his kitchens. No doubt they were getting ready to serve a meal fit for the latest princess of Silver Island. She had no intention of being a temporary attraction. The reason she was here was to stake her claim to something much more important than that. Caviar and champagne counted for nothing if it lacked one simple ingredient. She wanted Stefano's respect. That was more important than any amount of cordon bleu cookery, and she intended to get it. Leaving her drink on the bar she strolled away to admire a piece of glass sculpture so that he would not see her smile.

'Do you know what I'd really like, if it's not too much trouble?'

'Dressed in silk and diamonds? Do you want me to offend your sense of decency?'

Regarding him with a cool, steady gaze she said slowly, 'I'll tell you what would make my evening complete. Something utterly simple. No distractions.'

'No oysters or asparagus?'

'Aphrodisiacs? I don't need them,' she said simply.

He laughed, but for the first time the amusement never reached his eyes. As he phoned through to the kitchen, Kira watched him with intense interest. Moving restlessly beneath her gaze, he showed her into the dining room.

'I'll bet you can't remember the last time you shared such a simple meal with a girl,' she said idly.

There was nothing half-hearted about Stefano's reaction.

"On the contrary, I'll never forget it.'

His tone was so strange Kira shot a quick look at him. In profile he had a gaunt, distracted look she had never noticed before. As she watched, he collected himself and added, 'She was a girl who knew her own mind, too. That's the reason she's not here to share all this, tonight.' He pushed a hand out to indicate the luxury surrounding them. Kira could not help thinking of the svelte, glamorous Chantal.

'Someone else who wouldn't stand for your womanising ways?' she said slyly. 'So that makes two of us.'

'No, only one.'

That must mean she won't put up with it, but he thinks I will! Kira thought indignantly.

She was about to spring to her own defence, but the words died on her lips. Something about the way Stefano abruptly turned his back on her warned her to keep quiet. He walked over to the long, highly polished dining table. Closing his long sensitive fingers around one of the chairs, he pulled it out for her to sit down.

'And now, no more questions. You accepted my invitation to dine, so it's up to me to play the part of charming host.' The tension drained from his voice as he watched her shimmer into her seat. Candles set in silver candelabra stood in the centre of the table. Stefano lit them. Instantly, a million sparkles danced over the diamonds at Kira's throat. The same cold fire ran over her silken dress. It melted the frown creasing Stefano's brow. She actually saw him catch his breath, and it was wonderful.

'Kira…you have never looked lovelier,' he murmured.

She couldn't answer. Deep in her heart she hoped it was true, and wished she could believe him. While she was preening in front of her mirror, the thought of him had transformed her. Now he was working his magic on her in living, breathing reality. She felt fantastic, and he was telling her she looked it, too.

I have to put a stop to this. Right now, Kira told herself desperately. She was only here to prove to herself that she could resist him, that this was an adult, business relationship only....

But when Stefano looked at her in that way, only the first part of her brave statement was true. Business was the very last thing on her mind. The idea of a hot, very adult relationship with Stefano pushed everything else out into the cold.

Only a discreet knock at the door saved her. Swift, sure staff presented dinner on silver dishes and the finest china plates. Kira barely noticed the food. She could think of nothing but the tussle between her body's needs and her common sense. Stefano was trouble; she knew it.

'This is spectacular!' she laughed as the waiters poured her a chilled glass of pinot grigio.

'My guests always enjoy the best.'

'Is this how you entertain all your women?'

'No.'

Kira paused and looked along the table to where he was sitting. He looked up and met her eyes.

'What's the matter?'

'Then what do you do?'

His puzzled frown was exactly that—puzzled. However hard Kira tried to be suspicious, she couldn't spot anything shifty in his expression.

'Why this sudden obsession with other women?' His gaze was equally searching.

'You said I was only the second woman to stand up to you.'

He laughed. 'Yes...' He paused, clearly turning something over in his mind. 'If you must know, each time you answer back you remind me of my little sister, Maria.'

'Oh…I thought you were comparing me to…'

Kira's voice sounded very small suddenly, as she became aware of how little she really knew this man. His eyes burned with cold fire.

'No. Never.'

Kira's mind worked with the speed of light. She pieced together enough hints to know this was a delicate area.

'Were you very close to your sister?' she risked, pretending to be busy with her meal.

'We were inseparable. We had to be, on the streets. She had no one else to protect her.'

He dropped his fork with a clatter. Kira looked up sharply. Elbows on the table, his fingers were netted in front of his mouth as though to stop any more words escaping.

'Maria was very lucky to have a brother like you looking after her,' she said, hoping to sidestep the awkward subject. Stefano was not so tactful.

'It was people like me who made the streets dangerous in the first place,' he muttered.

'I don't think so.' Kira tried to pacify him, but she was desperate to hear more. 'You must have been different, even then. You told me how you started your own business.'

'Maria's death was the only reason I changed.'

He stopped talking, and looked up to meet her eyes. He saw only sympathy and willingness to listen. Taking a breath, he continued, his voice hoarse and seeming to force the words out. It was the first time he'd told anyone the truth for more than twenty years. 'She was killed when a raid on a shop went wrong. She hadn't wanted to go—I convinced her, saying it was "for the good of the family." It was my fault. From that moment on I vowed to turn my life around, and I did.'

'Maria would be really proud of you now.'

Stefano exhaled so heavily all the candle flames fluttered.

'I'm not so sure. When I decided to go straight, I made a clean break. Since her funeral, I haven't spoken to any members of my family. I turned my back on them all when I abandoned that way of life. It was the only way to get out. The last time I saw any of them was when I was acting as a witness for the prosecution.'

Oh, why did I have to open my big mouth? Kira thought desperately. She wanted to reach out and comfort him, but didn't dare. Where would that lead for either of them? Placing her knife and fork carefully on her plate she hoped for inspiration. None came. Instead, Stefano sprang to his feet when he saw she had finished. Collecting the remains of their meal, he carried it out to the kitchen. Kira fought the impulse to follow him. She desperately wanted to apologise for raising the subject, hold him, share his pain and tell him everything would be okay. It was impossible. Stefano wasn't that sort of man. Expecting an agonising wait, she was relieved when he came back almost immediately with a confection of tropical fruit sorbets. They glittered like jewels set in crystal dishes.

'There are sponge cakes and wafers, too, in case you share Maria's appetite as well as her temper,' he told her, sounding perfectly normal. There was no trace of the anguish she expected. All the self-control was back in place. Astonished, Kira looked up into his gaze. He was expressionless again, but something in her questioning face seemed to relax him.

'You're right, Kira. There are plenty of things about my life of which Maria would be proud. I'd never thought of that until you said it.'

'Wasn't it obvious?' she said as he placed the delicious dessert in front of her.

'No. I'd genuinely never considered it. All I focused on was losing her, and then the rest of my family. I knew there had to be more to life than crime and handouts. I made myself master of my own destiny. Working gave me an outlet, and an escape. I channelled all my frustrations into learning as much as I could about my own city, and then other places, as I climbed the ladder to success. That single-minded toil dulled the pain, but it left an awful void. Maybe that's why I'm never satisfied.'

He drew back from her suddenly. 'I've never told anyone that before,' he added, with such an air of surprise Kira couldn't help smiling.

'Then thank you,' she said softly.

On impulse, she stood. Before either of them knew what was happening, she kissed him on the cheek.

Coming to her senses like a sleepwalker waking from a dream, she dropped straight back into her seat. Until a moment before, she had been ready to resist him. Now she didn't know how she felt. In that same instant, Stefano made her confusion worse. He reached out and squeezed her hand.

'Let's live in the present and future, not the past, Kira.'

With a final pat he left her side and went back to his seat at the far end of the table.

* * *

Much later, Kira lay back on one of the long, cream leather couches and felt a huge smile creep across her face. A threatened disaster was turning into the best evening she had ever spent. The rest of the night had passed in a glorious blur of conversation—the best kind. Sharing true thoughts and ambitions and dreams. She felt filled with utter happiness.

A sound from the doorway made her sit up quickly. Stefano stood there, coffee in hand, looking at her.

'I didn't mean to wake you,' he said softly. Suddenly the sensual tension which had been disguised with words drew taut again. His gaze was serious, clouded and full of desire.

'It's okay. I wasn't asleep.'

She stretched into a sitting position as he came towards her.

'You don't have far to go,' he said simply.

Kira watched him placing things on the glass surface beside her. He wasn't looking at her any longer, but her body jangled from his nearness. He turned his head suddenly and she was caught in his gaze, almost trembling.

'Kira, tonight has been fantastic. In fact, I can't remember a night like it.'

'Nor me.' She sighed. 'Before I met you, I was uptight all the time. You're quite a role model.' Taking the cup and saucer from his hands, she looked reflective. 'I really wish I could be like you all the time, Stefano.'

He chuckled and sat down a little distance away from her, cradling his coffee. 'What—cold, calculating and immune to human feeling?'

'You need a little of those qualities to really succeed

in business. Loss, and an unhappy childhood, forces that tough shell onto people. I know all about that.'

'I do, too—although your background is still a mystery to me.' He watched her sip her drink. 'I've got every qualification the school of hard knocks can deliver, but what can have been wrong with your childhood? You told me it was full of Cotswold Christmases.'

'I was the big problem in my childhood,' she told him glumly. 'My adoptive parents wanted a porcelain doll, but they ended up with me instead. I've always liked doing things. They simply wanted me to *be*. I've never been happy, acting the part of a dim ornament.'

'I can imagine.' He smiled with a warmth that encouraged Kira to open up a little more.

'But that's all in the past. Now I'm earning a decent living, my stepparents can forgive me anything—as long as I keep sending the cheques home.'

He grimaced. 'Maybe you're lucky to have a family to spoil?'

She wriggled around to face him as they sat together on the settee. 'I wish that was all they wanted.'

He leaned forward and lifted the plate of sweet treats up from the coffee table. As he offered it to Kira, she got a tantalising hint of his evocative aftershave. She breathed deeply, but despite the distraction could not resist a piece of crystallised pineapple. Stefano selected a strawberry dipped in dark chocolate before putting the plate back on the table.

'The problem is, settling debts comes right at the bottom of my stepparents' list of priorities. I can't bear to think of them being without heat, light or transport so I bail them out—at least in theory. In reality, they use most of my money to send more invitations around the country club.'

Stefano made lazy circles in his coffee with a silver teaspoon. 'Why don't you offer to settle their debts direct?'

Kira was aghast. 'What—go behind their backs? I couldn't do that!'

'Then you'll have to be tough with them, Kira, and say "no more,"' Stefano said sharply. 'It will hurt in the short term, but will end up saving you a lot of grief. I should know,' he finished darkly.

Kira rolled her lip, wishing she could take his advice. 'It's all right for you. You're always so self-assured.'

He looked at her long and hard before replying. 'You don't do so badly. In fact, I would say you are an unusually forthright woman. You were certainly very decided about our plans tonight.'

Kira laughed. 'I've told you before. I like simple pleasures. You can have too much of a good thing!'

'I know, but I never expected to find anyone who agreed with me.' He sipped his coffee in silence, and then slowly and deliberately put it down on the table. 'Am I one of your simple pleasures, Kira? Or too much of a good thing?'

Her eyes remained on his hand. He drew it back from his cup, and rested it lightly on his thigh.

She bit her lip. 'I don't know. I can't decide.'

He hitched his shoulders in a casual gesture. 'You accepted my invitation and came for dinner.'

'Maybe I shouldn't have done.'

'Yes, you should, and I know you enjoyed the evening. I did, too,' he said, so quickly that she couldn't possibly doubt it. But worrying was a tough habit to break.

'Are you sure, Stefano?' she asked uncertainly.

'I'm positive.'

Her willpower started to wobble. Nothing had happened…so far. When Stefano seduced her the first time, it had simply been physical, if spectacular. Now, having spent the evening with such a sweet, funny, charming man, she was terribly worried. If he loved and left her after this, she would never be able to bear it.

'I'm not sure at all. I can't trust my own judgement any more, Stefano,' she confessed. Surely it was best to tell him the bad news straight out. 'I give money to lost causes. I made a fool of myself over a man and got my name all over the papers as a result. It was hell, and I'm so afraid of it happening again.'

The words escaped from her in a rush. She looked down at her lap, stunned to hear herself speak the words she had held back for so long. Beside her, she sensed Stefano tense. Her fingers twisted painfully as she waited for the questions to start.

'It's no wonder you send out mixed messages,' he said quietly. 'I wanted you from the moment I spotted you from the helicopter. When you put up barriers, I held back. Normally, I'd simply walk away, but something about you keeps me coming back. What happened? Tell me.'

His concern was so genuine. Kira was touched. Still staring at her hands, she spoke in the hope that sharing her pain might soften it somehow. 'I made an idiot of myself while I was at university. If I'm honest I knew there was something wrong about Hugh Taylor from the start. He only gave me his mobile number, saying he didn't have a landline at home. We never went back to his place, which should have been the decider. When I discovered he was married, I was too weak and stupid to drop him like the rat he was. To my shame I let the affair limp on, but I didn't know the half of it. It was left to his poor wife—or rather, one of them—to expose his double life. He was already a bigamist when he moved to Oxford, and started on me. The story was horrible enough to make the papers, and ruin me.'

There. She had said it. All the shame and embarrassment rushed over her again. She covered her face with her hands, unable to bear Stefano's gaze and sure she would never be able to look him in the eyes again after this.

'I was such a fool…' she went on through her fingers. 'I'd led such a sheltered life. I didn't know any better and took his bait. To know everyone was talking about me behind my back was awful. And my stepparents won't let it rest, even now…. There was no way on earth I could have carried on with my course after that. The shame was unendurable.'

Oblivious to everything but her pain, she had been rocking backwards and forwards. It was only when a light touch fell on her shoulder that she came to her senses. When Stefano spoke, she almost lost them again.

'How could anyone treat you like that?' he whispered.

'It's what people do. They use you, and then walk away,' she muttered, overwhelmed by the grubby scandal of it all.

'Yes. Life is hard for the weak.' Stefano's voice cut through the silence like a knife.

Kira dropped her hands and turned a simmering stare directly on him. If there was one thing she found more painful than self-hatred, it was someone else's pity.

'I am *not* weak,' she said, with absolute conviction.

'I know.' His reaction was equally unexpected. 'I was blaming myself for things I did, long ago. Seeing you like this has made me put my own past under the microscope. It isn't pretty,' he said grimly.

'You aren't a bit like Hugh!' She frowned.

'I was. I am,' he persisted. 'I may not have deceived my lovers—we had fun, but that was the extent of it. Sometimes I know I have left broken hearts behind me through not resisting temptation. You knew that when we slept together, didn't you?' he looked for her agreement.

'Yes. I'm under absolutely no illusions about you, Stefano,' she agreed. An odd expression flashed in his eyes for a moment, but then he continued.

'That's just as well. While I was on the streets I saw too many relationships driven apart by abuse and desperation. I was determined not to be like that, so I've never made any promises I can't keep. Giving a woman overwhelming pleasure is one thing. Promising to bind myself exclusively to her—never.'

'I understand.' Kira nodded. 'For me, you've always been Stefano the Seducer. Nothing more—and most definitely nothing less.'

The crease between his brows deepened a fraction.

'It almost sounds as though you approve of what happened between us, Kira.'

Unable to stop her memories warming her voice, she smiled. 'I can't help it. I do.'

Stefano's frown eased, and she corrected herself quickly.

'That is…I mean…I did.'

'You don't sound very sure?'

Slowly, almost hesitantly, his hand moved towards a curl of her hair that had strayed out of place. Coiling it over her shoulder, he smiled.

It was her turn to frown. 'I'm not.'

'Then let me help you to make up your mind. What you mean is, that as long as we are both completely honest with each other, no one will get hurt. Is that right?'

She nodded.

'I'm not sure I agree,' he said softly, shaking his head. Then his voice dropped to a whisper. 'For example, if I told you now that my deepest desire was to take you to bed, and you said that was the last thing you wanted to do, I would be crushed. Absolutely.'

His hand was still hovering near her hair. His eyes were very blue and clear.

Kira could barely breathe. She tried to speak. 'B-but then, if I said that, I would be lying…' she began, but could not finish.

Stefano anticipated what she was going to say. With the urgency she craved so much, he reached out and brought her within the circle of his arms. She could offer no resistance, and didn't want to. Stefano drew her towards him until their lips met in a kiss that swept away all her worries. She relaxed into the delicious warmth of his embrace. While his kiss held her captive, he drew his hand slowly up over her ribcage. As his fingers brushed the curve of her breast she shivered with anticipation.

'That is exactly the type of persuasion that can lead a girl astray,' she murmured.

'I know. Now, where would you like me to lead you—to your place, or mine?' he whispered, lifting her into his arms.

CHAPTER TEN

STEFANO undressed her right down to the diamonds. With a huge moon riding the velvet night outside, he worshipped his goddess of the flowers. 'I said you would be perfection, framed in honey orchids and silhouetted against the tropical sky,' he breathed, and it was true. He could not get enough of her, his lips sipping kisses from the yielding softness of her skin.

He made love to her the whole night long. No sensation was too divine. She fuelled feelings within him he had never experienced before. Each time she moved beneath his hands, a possessive need made him hold her ever more tightly to his body. He could not let her go. As their bodies entwined in a vibrant search for satisfaction, a truth began to slip in and out of the shadows shielding his mind. He had never before found such a perfect fit for his body, his mind and his senses. Kira had to be his for evermore. He wanted her—but his feelings ran far deeper than mere sex. He had wanted plenty of women in the past, and taken them all. But Kira was different. She was an experience he could not afford to lose.

Much, much later, Stefano swam back to consciousness through warm waves of satisfaction. Then the gravity of his feelings pulled him back to real life. Something incredible had happened last night. His seduction hadn't gone as planned; it had been spontaneous and reckless in a way he had never experienced before. The realisation opened his eyes wide. Then two words hurtled back at him and he shut them again, fast.

Love me.

Had he really said that? No, it wasn't possible. He wouldn't have—couldn't have—said it. He'd never done such a dangerous thing in his entire life. Although...he definitely remembered those words pulsating through the heat of his passion. Twice, in quick succession.

He must have imagined it. Yes, that was it.

With an exhalation of relief, he opened his eyes again. The room was still close and shadowy in the purple light before dawn. The sun outside had not risen high enough to penetrate the trees sheltering their refuge. He moved to check his wrist, but it was bare. He had tossed his watch aside in case it rubbed harshly against Kira's delicate skin. It was the first time he had ever done something like that, too. He wondered idly what time it was, but found he didn't care. Kira wouldn't mind, either. She liked it here on Silver Island as much as he did. They had lain awake for hours, listening to the mournful night birds outside, and wondering about the bright star that flickered down at them through the jalousie slats.

He tried to move, but couldn't. He had fallen asleep with Kira wrapped protectively in his arms. Until she wanted to escape, he was trapped.

Escape... The word rang through his head like an alarm.

Suddenly he stopped wanting Kira to wake. More

memories were racing back to taunt him. Before the wonderful abandon of bed, they had talked about her past last night—and his. That would mean she could never look at him in the same light again. Her image of him would be tainted by what she knew about his past. When she woke and gave him that lovely smile, what would be going on behind those beautiful eyes? His heart began to race. What exactly had they talked about last night, before words became unnecessary? He dimly remembered saying something about life being hard for the weak. Him? Weak? A hot wave of resentment washed over him, throwing more conversational flotsam back in his face. He had admitted turning his back on all his relatives. This, after Kira had been desperate to believe in some idealised dream of Italian family life. Well, he had shattered that illusion beyond repair!

Talking after sex, stargazing… Stefano was losing count of the number of firsts he had shared with Kira last night. There was no knowing where all this might lead, but he had his suspicions. Mercifully, another memory came back to him. He had stressed his independence again to her, hadn't he? She must understand that by now. Surely a man who could abandon his family couldn't be expected to be faithful to anyone else. In any case, where women were involved, Stefano considered himself a hunter, not a pet. Kira knew he was a lone wolf. Animals like that walked alone.

Beside him, she moved in her sleep. It was a luxurious movement, stretching out across the bed and freeing him.

A wolf walks alone, Stefano told himself. He hadn't been backed into a corner by anyone since he was a child.

Taking his chance, he began inching his way towards the edge of the bed. He had to escape. Last night, Kira had seen past his act of emotionally detached, successful businessman. She had captured some of his spirit. If he stayed by her side any longer, she would surely consume the rest.

He had to go. Now.

Peeling his body away from the last temptations of her touch, he eased his legs over the edge of the bed and inched into a sitting position. His clothes were scattered all over the place. As he reached for them, he tried not to think of the spectacular passion he had shared with Kira only hours earlier. Pulling his still-buttoned shirt on over his head, he stood, stifling a sigh of relief—but not well enough.

The rhythm of Kira's breathing changed. Stefano froze. So did she—and then she rolled over to greet him with that smile….

He swung away, unable to look her in the face.

'Stefano? What are you doing? It's too early to get up.'

Her voice was as velvet smooth as the touch he could never risk experiencing again. He shook his head.

'I'm sorry, Kira. I—I have to go. It's business. An urgent call. You know…' His voice disappeared. When Kira sat up and the silken sheet slipped away from her stunning nakedness, his willpower almost followed his voice.

'I never heard anything?'

'My phone was on vibrate. I really didn't want to wake you,' he added, with a sudden attack of the truth.

'So tell me—what is so important that it can pull you out of my arms?'

'You don't want to know.' Stefano went on dragging on his clothes.

'Yes, I do. Everything you do interests me, and I don't know the first thing about your work. All you've told me about so far is your past.'

He stopped and stared at her.

'Dio! Forget that. I shouldn't have said anything,' he muttered hurriedly. 'I—wanted to see how you'd react if I shot your dream of Italian family life down in flames. It was nothing. Forget everything I've told you.'

'No!' With a giggle she reached out to him, ready to tug him back into bed with her. 'First you try and sneak off without waking me, now you're backtracking on everything else as well. What's the matter, Stefano?'

He leapt back as though her touch was a threat. 'I've told you. It's nothing.' Making his face as bland as possible, he stared at her, daring her to contradict him. 'I must go.'

Kira had stopped laughing. The silence that fell between them now was deadly. There could be only one reason for his sudden coldness. He was leaving her. She gazed at him, unable to quite believe it.

'Why are you going? Tell me. I want to know.' Her voice crackled with emotion.

Stefano reached for his jacket and pulled it on. With short, sharp movements he checked that it contained his keys and wallet. 'All right—if you insist. I'm not going to lie to you, Kira. Have you thought you might not be the only one who could have second thoughts about all this?'

There was frostbite in his voice.

'It sounds like you're getting ready to abandon me.' Her voice barely trembled, but the tension was there.

'Of course that's what you must think.' Stefano's reply ricocheted back like a bullet. 'After what you've been through, it's only natural.'

Kira watched him brace himself, and take a step towards the bed. If kissing her goodbye took such a visible effort, she didn't want it. She sat back on her heels, distancing herself from him.

'Can you blame me, Stefano, when all men are so alike? I thought last night was something exceptional, but now it turns out every move you made, every word you spoke, was fiction,' she snapped.

Stefano drew back. The rising sun outside lit a shimmering aura around him. Despite the growing dawn, no bird or insect dared disturb the horrible silence as he formed his next argument. 'That's not true. But don't say you've never felt the need to nip a situation in the bud, before things get out of hand?'

She could hardly believe what she was hearing. Clutching the sheet against her body like a shield, she tried to make sense of this sudden change in him.

She was losing him. Unable to think of anything she had done or said to make him cool so abruptly, she began to panic.

'What is it? What can possibly have changed between us since last night, Stefano?' she implored.

'Nothing…and everything.'

His face was hard with an alien emotion. Kira gazed at him. The man who had seduced her with soft words and intoxicating caresses stared back at her in bitter disillusion.

'My US agent rang with details of an ideal investment property in upstate New York. That's where I'm going,' he said at last, each word drawn out and hesitant.

Kira's heart leapt. For a moment things didn't seem so bad. Looking around Sir Ivan's old house with Stefano had been wonderful. Maybe she could persuade him to include her in this next invitation? Her excitement was quashed by his next words.

'I'm leaving right away to go and view it. You can stay on here for as long as you like. Just tell one of my pilots when you want to go home.'

'So…you're flying to America alone?' Kira said slowly. With heart-rending effort, she managed to stop her smile sliding straight into despair.

He nodded. Grabbing his phone from the bedside table he dropped it into a pocket. Motionless with shock, Kira could not do or say a thing. It didn't matter. Stefano was perfectly prepared to do the talking for both of them.

'When I want to get away from people, I get right away from them. Once you've finished checking out Silver Island, you can go back to living in the grounds of Bella Terra, and working at my town house in Florence. While you're doing all that and flitting from one place to another, I'll keep well out of your way, until you've finished.'

'Why? There's nothing to stop you coming and going wherever you please. I'm won't be in your way,' Kira said, confused.

'I need space. I can't let you interfere with that.' Stefano's voice soared through the silence that fell between them.

It wasn't just a statement, it was a warning. Kira didn't need to be told twice. Gathering up her last reserves of courage, she stared him out.

'Don't worry on my account, Stefano. You know I'm

happier alone,' she said brusquely. 'I'll be fine. Once I leave here, I'll be totally absorbed by the Florence project. Go and find yourself another new house. Maybe you'll have better luck turning that one into a home, although I very much doubt it.'

'I can hope,' he said coolly.

'It won't take me more than a few hours to do my preliminary checks here. I'd be grateful if you'd arrange for me to be flown home this afternoon,' Kira countered, turning to hide her rage and shame as she got out of bed. Wrapping the sheet tightly around her body she stalked towards the bathroom. Ice-cold reserve was the only way she could deal with this situation. She expected Stefano to agree to her demand without question. His reaction came as a shock. As she strode past him, he grabbed her by the elbow.

'No. Stay here, on the island.'

'What?'

'That way I'll know where you are.'

'Now, wait a minute!' Kira flared. 'I may be on your payroll, but that doesn't mean you're in charge of my schedule. When it comes to my work, everything has to be done in the right order.'

And first on the list is getting you right out of my system, she thought painfully.

'I've got so much admin work to do back at home, I'll need to get started on it as soon as possible,' she went on, pulling her arm roughly from his grasp. 'Then there's the prince's project to sign off, and that's before I've even thought of starting work on your town house....'

Hugging the sheet tightly to her body, she started for the shower again. Hearing Stefano take some quick steps in pursuit and knowing that if he laid another hand on her she would be lost, she turned to confront him. She didn't want his touch clouding her judgement.

His expression gave her another jolt. He looked white-faced, almost lost, and as far from the smooth, composed Stefano as she had ever seen him. A moment later, and he was impenetrable once more.

'I'm glad you'll be keeping yourself busy,' he said, with all the passion of a diplomat.

Kira met his chilly good manners with a hard frost of her own. 'Don't talk about my work as though it is a hobby, Stefano. I signed that contract for you, don't forget.'

Her glare drew down shades over his expression. Any softening of his manner was instantly hidden from her, and from the world.

'How could I?' he said bitterly.

Stefano stormed away from Silver Island. He didn't need his newest employee lecturing him, even if her name was Kira Banks. Her anger worked away at his pride like a mountain stream running over rocks. An endless loop of her words went around and around in his head, and worse still, for the first time ever, Stefano could not settle to work on the plane journey. He hardly heard a word his agent said as they drove towards his latest dream property. His mind was a complete mess of regret and confusion. What did he want with another soulless palace? None of the others had brought him a moment's happiness or satisfaction. He had found both in Kira's arms, and then turned his back on her. Where was the sense in that? All he needed in his life was Kira, and her homely touch. Why had he ruined his only chance of happiness by letting slip his murky past, and the way he had abandoned his family? It would only reinforce her picture of him as a shallow pleasure seeker, flitting from one set of values to another. Kira deserved better than that, and she knew it.

She wouldn't want him now.

He barely noticed the colonial mansion he had travelled thousands of miles to inspect. Unable to make a decision on it, he retreated to Manhattan. His apartment on Fifth Avenue was as cheerless as any of his other homes. He roamed about, trying to put Kira out of his mind. It was hopeless. From the contrast between her cosy little home and his soulless apartment to the sight of lovers strolling hand in hand through Central Park, everything reminded him of her.

Finally, he went out, throwing himself into the surf of crowds and noise swirling through the city streets. It was supposed to block thoughts of Kira with the white noise of chaos. It didn't work. Each woman he saw was automatically matched against her memory, and found wanting.

Eventually, he washed up at an all-night club. The atmosphere was intended to stifle Kira's memory. Instead, her voice echoed in his brain. It cut straight through the racket, as he remembered how she had chosen to spend the evening with him on Silver Island—no distractions—rather than be wined and dined in the city. They wanted the same things out of life. Why didn't he trust himself to share them with her? The answer to that circled him like a shark but he didn't want to face it. Instead, he told himself that he'd done the right thing. She had been hurt before, and he'd only hurt her again—he had left her to protect her.

After a sleepless night, he went into the Manhattan

offices of Albani International. That was another disaster. He lasted twenty minutes. Unable to work, he spent the whole time resisting the urge to pick up the phone and ring Kira. In the end, he had to walk out and ask a secretary to order a car for him. He couldn't trust himself to make one simple, innocent business call. Once he lifted that receiver, he knew he would end up ringing Kira instead.

Kira tried to make a full and detailed assessment of Stefano's tropical paradise. It was impossible. She made some silly mistakes, and couldn't complete the simplest calculations. Her emotions were too raw. He had swept her up to heaven, and then dropped her the morning after. It was history repeating itself, and she felt empty, completely crushed. As soon as she had filled a few pages of her notebook, she made arrangements to board one of his private jets and leave the island chain.

The flight home was agonising. She did her best to make it look as though she was enjoying every second. She had a lifetime's experience of putting on a good show. She watched a romantic comedy, and took care to laugh in all the right places. She smiled and chatted to the cabin crew, and ate every meal and titbit they offered her. In contrast, she took only a solitary glass of white wine with her dinner, and most of that went back to the galley untouched. No way was she going to let anyone think Stefano Albani had driven her to drink!

One of his fleet of cars was waiting for her at the airport. The chauffeur said he had instructions to whisk her straight back home to La Ritirata. Kira had other ideas. She asked to be taken directly to Stefano's town house in Florence. That would put some distance between her and the valley she had left with such high hopes, only a couple of days before. Stefano had already infused the entire Bella Terra estate with so many memories for her. They had talked and laughed there. His new town house did not mean quite so much to her. As long as she kept well away from the place where he had seduced her, it had no hold over her. Stefano's offer to let her stay there while she worked on the project had seemed wildly overgenerous. Now she was glad of the opportunity. A break from La Ritirata was exactly what she needed. It would give her some time away from his memory.

Stefano suffered through another sleepless night, and that morning he knew he had to come to his senses. He couldn't think of anything but Kira and there could be only one outcome. He wanted her, and he would never get any rest until she was safely in his arms again. He didn't need to think any further than that. Summoning a car, he headed straight for the airport. Then he blazed a trail across the world. He hadn't thought beyond the fact that Kira had bewitched his mind and his body, and he could not live without her for a moment longer. All he wanted to do was reach her side. This was such a new sensation he had no idea what he was going to say, but right now, he didn't care. He needed her. The moment he saw her, the words would come. He knew it.

Driving towards the Bella Terra villa felt like coming home. It reinforced all his deepest feelings. This was where he wanted to spend the rest of his life. Now he was going to claim the woman he wanted by his side for all eternity. Leaping out of the car before his chauffeur had brought it to a standstill, he strode straight across the valley towards La Ritirata. He still hadn't worked out his argument, but words could wait. His first kiss would tell Kira all she needed to know.

He was so consumed by what he would do, it took him a while to realise something was wrong. The day was hot and the sky stormy, but all the windows of Kira's little home were tightly closed. As he registered that fact, he smelled smoke. The countryside was dry as dust. Fire was a constant threat, but now he saw it was a reality. Smoke was curling up from the back of La Ritirata. He started to run.

'Kira!'

Pulling out his phone as he ran, he summoned help from the villa but didn't wait for it to arrive. The woman he loved was in danger. Kicking down the front door, he burst into the living room. It was a furnace, centred on the burning kitchen door. A thick haze of smoke rose to fill the house, but Stefano never hesitated. Dropping to the floor where the atmosphere was clearest, he made straight for the burning room.

'Kira!'

There was no reply. He held his breath. The kitchen was well alight, but empty. His heart started to beat again. There was still hope. Calling her name, he quartered the living room, searching through the smoke and straining to hear the smallest noise. The crumble and crackle of feasting flames threatened to silence everything in its path.

Time was slipping away, dragging a suffocating chain ever tighter around his chest. He cast a desperate look at the fresh air outside, but could not waste a precious second. Reaching the staircase he went up on all fours. Keeping his head below the level of the smoke was good in theory, but the fire was sucking all the available

oxygen from the air. If Kira was here, he had to get her
out within the next couple of minutes. He ran into her
bedroom, his movements now desperate Walking away
from her was the worst mistake he had ever made, and
if he had now lost her for ever…

The town house in Florence was every bit as tempting as
Kira remembered from her first visit but the unfinished
business with Stefano hung over her like a thundercloud.
Nothing could distract her. Flipping on the TV, she tried
to get interested in the news. Gazing out of the window,
she was only half listening to the babbled headlines. The
sky outside was crying. She stared out over the sodden
rooftops of Florence. If only Stefano had not tried to shut
her out of his life so abruptly. She might still be lying
in his arms. The silver sand would be soft and warm
beneath their skin, while sunlight danced in patterns
overhead, sparkling through palm leaves.

   Here in Italy, it was wet and Kira was miserable. She
closed her eyes and inhaled, imagining the warm, fertile
perfume of her garden back at La Ritirata after a shower.
All it needed to make her fantasy complete was Stefano.
He had broken her heart, but she could not stop yearning for him. Angry with herself for being so weak she
reached over to switch off the useless distraction of the
television when her hand froze in midair. Half a dozen
words snatched her attention and held it, breathless.

   'Mystery fire rages at billionaire's hideaway…'

   The plasma screen was alive with flames and thick
funnels of smoke. As the presenter droned on, the scene
changed. A bird's-eye view showed again the frighteningly familiar landscape. The pictures were so huge and
horrific she could practically feel the heat. The news

report said only that a house on the estate of a reclusive billionaire had been destroyed, but Kira didn't need any more details. Despite the flickering flames and jagged camera work, she recognised La Ritirata.

Her home had been destroyed.

Alight with fear, she called a hire car and drove straight to the Bella Terra estate. The smell of smoke was almost overpowering as she drove up the track towards the villa. She had to close all the ventilators. It was impossible to miss the turning for La Ritirata. The TV item had been recorded earlier in the day, so the news crews and fire services had vanished. Only the mess remained, where all their vehicles had been stationed. Grass and bushes were flattened, and the recent rain had surrounded the blackened stinking ruins of her little house with mud.

Kira put a hand up to open her car door, but stopped before she made contact. She couldn't do it. She couldn't step out into this disaster. Unable to bear the horrible sight any longer, she turned the car around and headed for Stefano's villa. The sick feeling inside her was made a hundred times worse by the reek of smoke that crept into the vehicle. There could be no escape from the after-effects of the blaze. They would linger for a long time, and in her memory for ever.

She brought her car to a halt on the grand terrace where Stefano had once parked his helicopter. She got out of the car, and plodded up the steps to the great front doors. There she pulled on the bell, which echoed like an alarm through the rambling old house. She purposely kept her back to the wreckage of La Ritirata, unable to look at the damage.

When the villa door opened, the interior came as

a complete surprise to her. It had been transformed. Although Stefano had owned La Bella Terra for only a few days, an impressive desk and banks of telecommunications equipment had already been installed in the reception area. As Kira stepped inside, a woman rushed forward and grabbed her hands. Her face was tight with panic and stress and it took a few moments for Kira to recognise Stefano's senior PA beneath the smudges of mascara. That was a shock. Kira had last seen her arriving on Silver Island, and assumed she would have followed her boss to the USA.

'Is there any news, Miss Banks?'

'What about? And why are you here?' Kira stared at her, puzzled, the chaos surrounding her house momentarily pushed to one side. 'I thought you stuck to Stefano like a Post-it note?'

At the mention of her boss the woman went even whiter.

'Oh, I am so sorry, Miss Banks…'

Feeling panic rise, Kira prised herself out of the PA's grasp. To be clutched at by a stranger was almost as bad as seeing her house in ruins.

'It's only sticks and stones,' she muttered, embarrassed by such a show of emotion from someone she hardly knew. Stefano mustn't be allowed to see her fail. If she could walk away from him on Silver Island, she could carry on holding everything together now. She avoided thinking in too much detail about how much she had lost. All of her hard work over the years…

'It isn't as though there were lives at stake,' she went on, keeping a skin of ice over the turbulent depths of her true feelings. 'Could you send a message to Signor Albani, please?' she asked briskly. 'I was only going to be staying in Florence while I worked on his town house, but now I've lost my home, I've got nowhere to live. I'll need to stay in town on a permanent basis, until I can sort things out….'

The girl was looking at her in confusion.

'Miss Banks! You mean to say you don't know what happened? Signor Albani has been rushed to hospital!'

Kira's mind went completely blank. She fell back, aghast.

'He tried to save your house. He put his life on the line, looking for you, and for what? You hardly seem to care about him, or your home!' The PA was clearly fighting tears.

Kira was suddenly aware of the villa's entrance hall filling with faces. Builders, architects and members of staff poked their heads from doorways or looked over the banisters from the upper floors. Covered in shame, she wanted to run away and hide, but she was too thunderstruck to do anything but gawp at the collection of furious, accusing faces.

'Me? What have I done?' she said faintly. 'It's not my fault!' No answer came. The PA had turned away and Kira was left to her own thoughts. If Stefano had not gone looking for me—*why was he looking for me?*

'I had no idea he was in the country. I thought he was still in America,' she whispered to herself.

Kira's heart solidified inside her chest. Stefano had left her, that last fateful day on Silver Island. He had betrayed her, forcing mental and physical distance between them. Now she was expected to believe he had taken a pointless risk by searching for her in an empty house! It was too much to take on board.

Ignoring her audience, she marched straight back out to her car. On the way, she steeled herself to take another glance at the smoking ruin that had once been her home. It was terrifying. Stefano had been in there. She had to find out why.

CHAPTER ELEVEN

ONCE at the hospital, rules and regulations held her up for ages. Getting into Stefano's private suite took longer than the drive from La Bella Terra had done. When she was finally allowed to enter, her nerves were put to their stiffest test. Stefano lay motionless in the bed. His eyes were closed, and the only colour in his face came from a network of cuts, scratches and bruises. His natural colour had drained away to a deathly grey. Once the orderly had shown her into the room, he left. When she was completely alone with the patient, Kira could not contain herself any longer. She rushed forward and grabbed his hand, which was swathed in bandages.

'Stefano!' she gasped.

He flinched, scowled and opened his eyes, in that order. Kira instantly dropped his hand and stepped back, his cold eyes reminding her of the distance between them.

'What are you doing here? I gave express instructions that you, above all people, weren't to be allowed in.'

Digging both elbows into his bed, he struggled up into a sitting position. Once there, he reached for the alarm button on his side table.

'Stop! Don't blame the staff. It's nobody's fault but

mine,' Kira said. 'I waited until the shift changed on reception and then said I was one of your PAs, coming to consult you about some paperwork.'

Stefano let his hand fall back to the bed, winced and then managed a half-smile at her ingenuity.

'Why do you think I issued that order? I didn't want you to see me like this.' He wouldn't meet her eyes.

There was a silence. Scrabbling for words, Kira said with an awkward laugh, 'I did all that work making my house beautiful and comfortable, but never got around to fitting a sprinkler system!'

'Dio! It was a country cottage, not the Uffizi Gallery.' They both paused again.

'Are your burns very painful?'

He looked at her finally, but only for a moment. 'They're not too bad. I'm only in for observation.'

Kira poured him a glass of water, but he shook his head.

'Why did you risk going into a burning building?' she burst out, unable to wait any longer.

For a moment she thought he wasn't going to answer her, but then he sighed and spoke.

'I thought you were inside. I assumed you would shut yourself away in La Ritirata after getting back from Silver Island.'

Kira watched him intently. He brushed folds from his coverlet, picked up his watch from the bedside cabinet and put it on, but he did not look directly at her.

'So...you actually went looking for me?' she said at last.

'It was the least I could do,' he said, still avoiding her eyes. 'I realised that, however much you claimed to understand I wasn't offering you anything more than a good time, I had hurt you. I was determined to make up for that. I saw smoke, thought the worst and broke in. I thought maybe you were asleep, or unconscious, or...'

'You risked your life for me,' Kira said slowly. 'I never imagined anyone would do that.'

'I couldn't help myself.' Stefano evaded her eyes. 'The flames took hold very quickly. When I realised you weren't there I concentrated on getting as many of your belongings out as possible.'

'You saved some of my things!' Kira's heart leapt for a moment, before shock distracted her. 'You stayed and did all that when I wasn't even in the house, Stefano?'

'They were your things. You made a perfect home. You weren't going to lose anything, if I could help it,' he said simply. 'Things matter to you.'

And so do you, she thought painfully.

Shutting her eyes, she sank down in the nearest chair. When Stefano first abandoned her, she had been filled with anger. That evaporated the second she heard he had been injured. Now she felt weak, confused and resentful that he should force her through such an obstacle course of emotions.

'You might claim to know my mind, but you're a total mystery to me, Stefano Albani. I thought you didn't ever want to see me again. And then you go and do something like this,' she said quietly.

'I've told you. I couldn't help myself.' Stefano sounded as though he could hardly believe it himself.

Kira did not need to search his face to see that he was telling the simple truth.

'Did you buy that house in America?'

He shook his head. 'It didn't seem important any more. Once upon a time I had nothing, but now I can have what I like, and make a home anywhere I want. It's enough to know that. I don't need to follow through.'

'But you can't make yourself any kind of home, can you? That's what all this is about!' Her eyes flew open. 'On the day we first met, you spoke as though the Bella Terra estate was the answer to all your prayers. You were going to make your home there, and settle. But it wasn't good enough, was it? I should have seen the warning signs when you showed me around the town house in Florence—that must have been your previous "ideal home." It would have been the solution to all your problems—until you lit upon my valley. Before that, it must have been Silver Island. All these places have one thing in common, Stefano. You haven't been able to make a home out of any of them!'

Breathless, she ran out of words. Stefano had watched her in silence. Now he laced his fingers together, winced and straightened them carefully again before speaking.

'We're alike, you and I. Neither of us likes to be out of control. Neither of us appreciates surprises.' He paused before adding, 'But my existence has been anything but predictable since I met you.'

His calculated tone was in such contrast to her outburst, Kira sat back in surprise. He seemed to have somehow retreated from her, in spite of not having moved from his bed.

'I'm a free agent, Kira.' He spread his hands in a bleak gesture. 'I need to be able to come and go, in the same way you do. Work defines both our lives, doesn't it? We can't devote ourselves to our careers if we're always looking out for the other, can we?' he finished, with a hint of defiance.

Over the past few days Kira had begun to reassess her life. She was beginning to think work was playing too big a part in it. Her heart sank as she realised that Stefano had clearly done no such thing.

He grazed his teeth over his lower lip. 'What are you going to do about La Ritirata now? I doubt if it's habitable.'

'There isn't much left standing.'

Always restless, Stefano reached for the water Kira had poured him. After taking a sip, he slid the glass across his bedside table. He did not look at her as he spoke.

'Look—don't take this the wrong way, Kira, but why not consider selling what is left of your house to me? I can take it off your hands, give you a good price and you can start again. I can make everything all right for you again. You were never keen on a stranger moving into Bella Terra. This way, it won't matter to you.'

Kira stared at him, looking for any trace of the man she thought she loved. All she could see was the cold, hard exterior. She forced herself to ask, 'You—you'd like me to go back to England? '

'Well, it's obviously up to you,' he responded mildly. 'I'm simply offering to help you. That heap of rubble is nothing but a liability to you now.'

The truth hurt. Kira was so used to it, she only knew one defence. She squared up to him again.

'A liability? You know all about those, of course. Apparently, that's how you saw me on the morning you abandoned me on Silver Island.'

She rose from her seat, all the hurt rushing back as fresh and raw as that first moment when she saw him getting ready to leave her.

'I served your purpose, and then you left.'

'Oh, Kira…' For a moment she thought she saw a flash of something deeper in his eyes, but then it was gone, and when he spoke again, his voice was carefully controlled.

'That night on Silver Island, you seemed to understand me better than I knew myself. You know what I'm like now, which is more than anyone else in the world does. I didn't want you to get too fond of me, so I went to look at a property. That's all.'

Kira looked at him, really looked at him. His white face and guarded eyes. He was lying. She knew it. Somewhere deep inside, he must know it, too. Her sadness was suddenly gone, eclipsed by anger at his stubborn blindness. Her hands flexed in impotent rage. 'You are a coward, Stefano. We had something incredible between us—I know you felt it, too. Deny it all you want, but I hope one day you'll understand what you have thrown away. Property? You've already got more of that than you know what to do with! Why don't you start looking closer to home, Stefano? Oh, I'm sorry, you don't have one of those!' Grabbing her bag, she threw herself towards the door.

'Wait, Kira! Where are you going?'

'I'm going to show you how to make a home from absolutely nothing, Stefano. I'm going to rebuild La Ritirata stone by stone, if it takes me the rest of my life,' she finished, with steely resolve.

Swinging out of his room, she let the door slam shut behind her.

Shell-shocked, Stefano dragged himself out of bed. He didn't want things to end like this. They needed to finish on his terms—he needed the last word. He flung open the door of his private room. She was already gone, straight out of his life. It was too late.

It was almost dark by the time Kira reached her car. With a heavy heart she decided there was no point in going back to La Ritirata until the morning. Nothing could be done by night. Instead, she headed back to her guest suite in Stefano's Florentine town house.

Hours later, she wished she had returned to the Bella Terra valley anyway. Sleep was impossible. Inspecting the ruins of her home by torchlight would have been a better use of her time than tossing and turning in bed. She got up while it was still barely light, and went out for a short walk around town. It was supposed to clear her head, but her mind was too full for that. She thought about the home she had lost, and how much more terrible it could so easily have been. Stefano might have been killed. When it came to matters of life and death, possessions didn't matter. They could be replaced. People couldn't. When he left her on Silver Island, Stefano had torn a hole in her heart. While he was still alive, there was a chance it might be repaired. If he had died in the fire, he would have been lost to her forever.

At least today she still had hope, where there might have only been tragedy.

Kira was a perfectionist, but when it came to Stefano's town house her standards reached new heights. She went into overdrive. When she wasn't busy with her contract to beautify the house, its roof and courtyard, she sat in her borrowed suite and co-ordinated the rebuilding of her own home. It was so painful to be confronted by the ashes of her happy life, but she refused to be beaten. Her vow to recreate her home was written in smoke-blackened stones. She poured all her anger and disappointment into her project to rebuild it. Each day she concentrated on her work at Stefano's town house, determined to fulfil her contract impeccably. Each evening, she drove to La Ritirata and worked on until it was too dark to see. She did all the odd jobs that might otherwise eat into the builders' time: making phone calls, sweeping up and washing down. Everything had to run according to her plan. Nothing must go wrong. She wanted her house to stand as a monument to her iron will.

Her commitment to both jobs never wavered. Her self-control often did. She was so glad that this was something she could do alone. For anyone else to see her anguish would have been unbearable. Each time she walked out onto Stefano's new roof garden, she kept expecting him to appear. He never did. As she walked through the cool, beautifully designed rooms of his suite, she knew that other women would have the benefit of the emperor-size bed and the shower that was big enough for two. She had lost him. Her bridges were burned, along with her house.

She had turned out to be the architect of her own unhappiness, and that was the most painful thing of all.

Kira's punishing schedule began to take its toll. There were times when she could barely drag herself from one project to the other. Her body was numb with exhaustion. She kept her mind blank with the anaesthetic of work. If she let it wander for a moment, it homed straight in on Stefano.

Rebuilding La Ritirata would take a long time, and more money than she could bear to think about. Her beloved garden was wrecked. It sagged beneath the weight of disaster. Nothing had escaped. Plants had been scorched, crushed beneath falling masonry or trampled and drowned by the emergency services or the builders.

Her house could be replaced, but its heart and soul would take a lot longer to repair. Wandering around the site, Kira couldn't help wondering if it would feel as soulless as all Stefano's properties did. There would be no love in it. She had none left to give. The rebuilt La Ritirata would rattle with emptiness, and smell of nothing but new paint and plaster. They were nice smells, but as impersonal as a hospital. The place would be eerily silent, too. Kira had grown to love the little creaks and moans her old house made. All its imperfections would vanish, like the original building. None of the new windows would jam, and the front door would open first time, every time. The usual pantomime of wiggling the key and bumping her shoulder against one particular spot would be a thing of the past. This new house should be ideal in every way, but somehow she knew it never would be. Something would always be missing.

All she had ever craved was a quiet life, far away from strangers, in her old house with its funny little ways. Now she had lost everything. Looking out across the valley at the Bella Terra villa, all Kira saw now was the wrong sort of isolation. She wanted to carry on being alone—alone, together with Stefano.

It was the end of her wonderful dream. She had lost her home, and the only man she would ever love or need or want. Stefano had been on to something. She

should have accepted his offer to buy the ruins of La
Ritirata. Her contracted jobs were well on the way to
being finished—they didn't need her any longer. There
was nothing in the Bella Terra valley for her now. Sadly,
regretfully, she pulled out her mobile phone.

He had been right all along. All she had to do was
tell him.

It was ironic. Stefano's problem was that he could never
be satisfied with what he had. Kira's problem was the
exact opposite. She loved what she knew, and never
wanted it to change.

Her message to him was a simple one: You've won.
I don't want to replace my home here after all.
You can have it.

It had been hard enough to begin. Finishing it took
forever. Every ending she added felt desperate, so finally
she put the single word Kira and pressed Send.

She had a long wait. Her time in Florence, which
should have been spent packing, kept being interrupted
by checking her email in-box. Each time she opened it
and there was no reply from Stefano, it felt like another
rejection. She usually spent her time avoiding office
work and the computer. Today was different. Finally,
eyes dry and gritty from staring at a screen that refused
to come up with the only name she wanted to see, she
flung herself away from the desk with a cry of desperation. Blindly, she dashed up onto the brand new roof
garden she had designed and built for him.

For as long as she could remember, gardens had
been Kira's sanctuary. That magic did not work today.
Solitude could not help her. She drifted around, unsee-
ing. Moving from the flower boxes of pelargoniums to

the terracotta pots of lemon trees and back again, she was locked inside her own thoughts. It was not a happy place to be. The only thing that could distract her was the idea Stefano might have replied to her email, and she had missed it. Within minutes of escaping from the screen, her nerve broke and she fled back inside.

Inevitably, she discovered her message had been answered almost as soon as she abandoned her laptop. Excitement plummeted to despair as she opened Stefano's message to find only an automatic response. He was going off-message until further notice.

Kira put both hands on the edge of the table and pushed herself back from her computer. That made his feelings pretty clear.

The rest of her day went to waste. She could not eat, or settle to anything for more than a few moments. As evening approached she gave up and drove to the Bella Terra valley. The place had always healed her in the past. It didn't happen today. Gazing at the foundations of the new house, she wondered if the next person to live in it would be truly happy there.

A chill breeze ruffled her hair. High in a nearby pine, an owl quavered its mournful cry. Cold weather would soon be on its way. One of Kira's great pleasures had been to feed the creatures driven close to her old home in winter. When she left, she would lose that. It would be a terrible wrench. She might hate this new house, but she still loved the Bella Terra valley.

On impulse, she decided to recreate some of the best things about her life at La Ritirata. She shook out some biscuit crumbs onto an upturned oil drum. Within seconds a robin returned to investigate. Gathering up small branches from beneath the trees, she began rebuilding

the wood pile. It would be ready for burning by next
winter. The memories of the sound and fragrance of
crackling wood might make this soulless new house feel
a little bit more homely. The new owners would enjoy
that.

She was kneeling on the ground, picking up pine
cones, when a sound made her whirl around in alarm.
What she saw almost stopped her heart.

'Stefano!'

Without waiting for her to say any more, he walked
across what had once been her garden. She froze. As
imposing as ever, his long shadow fell across her. Sitting
back on her heels, Kira tried to push her tumble of coppery gold hair behind her ears.

'Yes,' he said mildly. Reaching down, he brushed a
fragment of dried grass from the crown of her head. She
held her breath. He leaned back, carefully under control,
and she breathed again,

'You've lost weight,' she said faintly. He laughed.

'I've been too busy to eat. I've found a new purpose
in life.'

'That American property tempted you after all?' She
smiled, dying inside. He shook his head, but that gave
her no cause to hope. Instead, she became defensive.

'I've gone beyond the point of playing games, Stefano.
Did you get my email?'

'Yes. That's why I'm here.' He was equally forthright.

She watched him speculatively. 'Why hasn't your
office answered any of my messages?'

He flipped his keys into his pocket. 'They had nothing to tell you. They couldn't contact me. I was on my
way here.'

'Why? Of all the places in your empire, why visit here?' Kira asked, hearing her voice trembling slightly.

He paused for a long time before he answered. The only sound was the idle clink of coins in his pocket. It cranked up the tension to a point where Kira jumped when the lonely owl called again.

'I'm not visiting, Kira,' he said at last. 'I'm back in the valley for good.'

She stared at him, wondering what to ask and where to start. 'Until five minutes ago I knew exactly what I was going to do. I had everything planned. Now you've parachuted back into my life, and I don't know what to think.'

'So don't think anything.' He came towards her again with a huge, beautiful smile and she stood, legs wobbly, to meet him. 'Just feel. All you need to know is that your problems are over, tesoro.' He reached out for her and Kira took a hasty step back. Her body was already reacting to his presence, and she knew that if she let him take her in his arms all would be lost.

Anger bubbled up inside her. How dare he just return so casually? 'I don't think so, Stefano. I have a feeling they may only just be beginning. Do you think you can flit in and out of my life on a whim? You abandoned me once, remember? How do you expect me to trust that you won't suddenly change your mind again?'

Stefano's smile faded.

'I want to explain.'

'What is there to say? You deceived me!'

A lightning bolt of anger galvanised his body. 'That's not true, Kira, and you know it! We both said we wanted to resist mixing business and pleasure. When it happened and I made a move, you could have said no. I would have respected that. We are so alike, both wary of entanglement. We knew the dangers. That meant you were never under any pressure to respond, and neither was I.' He had started angrily, but the bitterness in his voice melted away as he added, 'But we did, and there can never be any doubt that you are a woman who knows exactly what she wants. I wanted the same thing,' he finished quietly. 'And I still want it.'

Kira bit her lip as her eyes threatened to fill with tears. His words had some truth to them. He had been cruel to her, but she had been naive. 'I always said I would never let myself be so vulnerable again,' she said eventually.

'I know, and that was why I had to leave!'

His words escaped in such an explosion, Kira's head jerked up.

'I told you too much about myself on our last night together, Kira. That's why you must have realised I'm not to be trusted.'

In the days they had been apart Kira had combed every magazine and newspaper, steeling herself to read about Stefano and a string of other women. There had been nothing.

'I don't know what you're talking about, Stefano,' she challenged him at last. 'And you can't possibly say something like that without following it up!'

'I don't know if I can,' he said, with difficulty. 'You learned more about me in those final hours than I have ever revealed to anyone else. Telling you about Maria and my family lifted a weight off my mind. At first it felt good. But next morning...' He shook his head wordlessly.

'I realised I had gone too far. I had to get away.'

Kira waited, hardly daring to breathe. It was a long time before he spoke again.

'I told you the darkest secret of my life—that in order to make myself a success, I turned my back on my birth family.'

'You also told me you chose honesty when you decided to leave them,' Kira said quietly.

He nodded, pushing a hand through his hair in a sharp, agitated gesture. 'But at the time…the thought of you discovering I couldn't be any more loyal than your faithless Hugh…it was too much to bear.' He exhaled in a rush. 'And knowing you knew my secrets, what my childhood was really like… I've never told anyone that since I escaped it. I kept imagining you looking at me with disgust or—far worse—pity.' He lowered his head for a moment, the sharp planes of his face tense and pale.

'Stefano,' Kira said softly. 'You must know your past could never make any difference to me. It made you the man you are now, the man I—' she stopped herself and swallowed hard before continuing '—I know. I understand exactly how you feel. I panicked after the first time we spent the night together. I couldn't believe how perfect it felt—there was no way I could trust it to last. I knew it would crush me when it fell, when you decided I wasn't good enough—or met someone else…'

'What changed your mind?'

Kira sighed. 'To be honest, I couldn't stay away from you! I wanted to keep my distance—but I didn't want to lose touch with you either. I think I was lost from the beginning, really. Ever since you gave me your business card, I've been treating it like a holy relic,' she finished ruefully.

'You wouldn't be the first,' he assured her.

They stood and looked at each other—and then they laughed.

Stefano reached out to her again, his touch gliding over her cheek. In that moment, Kira forgot all her fears. All she wanted to do was check that her body was still a perfect fit for his arms. Closing the gap between them, she looked up into his eyes. They were intense and totally focused on her face. His smile enclosed her in warm, honeyed security as his touch brushed like silk against her skin.

'I—I don't know what came over me when we made love on Silver Island, Kira. It was every bit as good—no, it was better than when we were in Florence. That was the problem. First I couldn't get you out of my mind, and then I didn't want to let you out of my bed. I'd never felt like that about any woman before. It was such an overwhelming experience, I had to get away. I thought I was lost. In fact, the exact opposite was true. Once we were apart I discovered you are my anchor in life, Kira. That's why I could never resist coming back to you. You're strong, and centred, and keep me grounded in real life. When I abandoned you on Silver Island, it was like leaving behind part of myself. It was the best part, but I knew it was safe with you because after we made love that night, something changed. I became one half of a couple. Do you realise what that means? Since then I've been lost without you, adrift. We are meant to be together, Kira. You make me whole. There can be no going back now—for either of us.'

She shook her head in disbelief. She had never dared

to hope that his feelings might run so close to hers. 'That's exactly the way I felt, after Florence,' she told him quietly. 'For the first time in my life, I didn't want to be alone any more. That scared me, because it felt so different.'

He nodded.

'The moment I left you on Silver Island, I discovered you were inescapable. I was carrying you everywhere. You were inside me—in my thoughts, and deep within my heart. I went back to find you in La Ritirata, but the fire got in the way. When you found me in the hospital, I couldn't find the words to tell you the truth—I was still scared. I drove you away again, stubborn fool that I am. When you left, I tried to convince myself it was what you wanted. That it was the right decision, and I tried again to let you go. But I was lying to myself. Kira, we need each other. Together, we can show the world what family really means. Together, we'll be unbeatable. That's why I came to find you. Kira, my only love, am I too late?'

He was gazing into her eyes, trying to read her thoughts. Kira feasted her eyes on him for a long time before replying, but there wasn't a doubt in her mind. 'Too late?' she said finally in a soft, slow voice. 'You can't be, for here I am.' Stefano's face lit up with blazing joy as he pulled Kira against him.

'And here you stay.' He cupped her face in his hands and passionately kissed her as she melted against him. 'With me, for ever.'

Coming Next Month

from **Harlequin Presents**®. Available January 25, 2011.

Coming Next Month

from **Harlequin Presents**® **EXTRA.** Available February 8, 2011.

REQUEST YOUR
FREE BOOKS!

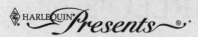

2 FREE NOVELS PLUS
2 FREE GIFTS!

YES! Please send me 2 FREE Harlequin Presents® novels and my 2 FREE gifts (gifts are worth about $10). After receiving them, if I don't wish to receive any more books, I can return the shipping statement marked "cancel." If I don't cancel, I will receive 6 brand-new novels every month and be billed just $4.05 per book in the U.S. or $4.74 per book in Canada. That's a saving of at least 15% off the cover price! It's quite a bargain! Shipping and handling is just 50¢ per book.* I understand that accepting the 2 free books and gifts places me under no obligation to buy anything. I can always return a shipment and cancel at any time. Even if I never buy another book, the two free books and gifts are mine to keep forever.

106/306 HDN E5M4

Name _____ (PLEASE PRINT) _____

Address _____ Apt. # _____

City _____ State/Prov. _____ Zip/Postal Code _____

Signature (if under 18, a parent or guardian must sign)

Mail to the **Harlequin Reader Service:**
IN U.S.A.: P.O. Box 1867, Buffalo, NY 14240-1867
IN CANADA: P.O. Box 609, Fort Erie, Ontario L2A 5X3

Not valid for current subscribers to Harlequin Presents books.

**Are you a current subscriber to Harlequin Presents books and want to
receive the larger-print edition? Call 1-800-873-8635 today!**

* Terms and prices subject to change without notice. Prices do not include applicable taxes. N.Y. residents add applicable sales tax. Canadian residents will be charged applicable provincial taxes and GST. Offer not valid in Quebec. This offer is limited to one order per household. All orders subject to approval. Credit or debit balances in a customer's account(s) may be offset by any other outstanding balance owed by or to the customer. Please allow 4 to 6 weeks for delivery. Offer available while quantities last.

Your Privacy: Harlequin Books is committed to protecting your privacy. Our Privacy Policy is available online at www.eHarlequin.com or upon request from the Reader Service. From time to time we make our lists of customers available to reputable third parties who may have a product or service of interest to you. If you would prefer we not share your name and address, please check here. ☐

Help us get it right—We strive for accurate, respectful and relevant communications. To clarify or modify your communication preferences, visit us at www.ReaderService.com/consumerschoice.

HARLEQUIN®

A *Romance*

FOR EVERY MOOD™

Spotlight on

Classic

Quintessential, modern love stories
that are romance at its finest.

See the next page
to enjoy a sneak peek from
the Harlequin® Romance series.

*Harlequin Romance author Donna Alward is loved
for her gorgeous rancher heroes.*

*Meet Wyatt as he's confronted by both a precious
little pink bundle left on his doorstep and his neighbor Elli
who's going to show him the ropes....*

Introducing
PROUD RANCHER, PRECIOUS BUNDLE

THE SQUAWKING QUIETED as Elli picked the baby up, and
Wyatt turned around, trying hard to ignore the feelings of
inadequacy as Darcy immediately stopped fussing.

"Maybe she's uncomfortable. What do you think, sweet-
heart?" Elli turned her conversation to the baby.

"What do you think is wrong?" Wyatt asked, putting the
coffee pot back on the burner.

A strange look passed over Elli's face, one that looked
like guilt and panic. But it was gone quickly. "I couldn't
say," she replied.

"But you were so good with her this afternoon." Wyatt
put his hands on his hips.

"Lucky, that's all. I just…remembered a few things."
The same strange look flitted over her features once more.

Wyatt took the coffee to the table. "You fooled me. You
looked like you knew exactly what you were doing." So
much so that Wyatt had felt completely inept. A feeling he
despised. He was used to being the one in control.

Elli and Darcy walked the length of the kitchen and
back. After a few moments, she admitted, "I haven't really
cared for a baby before. The things I thought of were simply
things I'd heard about. Not from experience, Mr. Black."

Her chin jutted up, closing the subject but making him

want to ask the questions now pulsing through his mind. But then he remembered the old saying—*Don't look a gift horse in the mouth.* He'd benefit from whatever insight she had and be glad of it.

"I don't really know what babies need," he said. "I fed her, patted her back like you did, walked her to sleep, but every time I put her down…"

Wyatt almost groaned. Of course. He'd forgotten one important thing. He'd been so focused on getting the formula the right temperature that he'd forgotten to check her diaper. Not that he had any clue what to do there either.

Pulling calves and shoveling out stalls was far less intimidating than one tiny newborn.

"She's probably due for a diaper change, isn't she." He tried to sound nonchalant. This was a perfect opportunity. Elli must know how to change a diaper. He could simply watch her so he'd know better for the next time.

Instead, Elli came around the corner of the counter and placed Darcy back in his arms. "Here you go, Uncle Wyatt," she said lightly. "You get diaper duty. I'll fix the coffee. Cream and sugar?"

Oh boy, Wyatt thought, looking down into Darcy's pursed face, his smug plan blown to smithereens. He was in for it now.

Will sparks fly between Elli and Wyatt?

Find out in
PROUD RANCHER, PRECIOUS BUNDLE

Available February 2011 from Harlequin Romance

Try these Healthy and Delicious Spring Rolls!

INGREDIENTS	DIRECTIONS
2 packages rice-paper spring roll wrappers (20 wrappers)	1. Soak one rice-paper wrapper in a large bowl of hot water until softened.
1 cup grated carrot	2. Place a pinch each of carrots, sprouts, cucumber, bell pepper and green onion on the wrapper toward the bottom third of the rice paper.
¼ cup bean sprouts	
1 cucumber, julienned	
1 red bell pepper, without stem and seeds, julienned	3. Fold ends in and roll tightly to enclose filling.
4 green onions finely chopped— use only the green part	4. Repeat with remaining wrappers. Chill before serving.

Find this and many more delectable recipes
including the perfect dipping sauce in

YOUR BEST BODY NOW
by
TOSCA RENO
WITH STACY BAKER

Bestselling Author of
THE EAT-CLEAN DIET®

Available wherever books are sold!